REBEKAH - GIRL DETECTIVE
FIFTH GRADE MYSTERIES

BOOKS 1-8

PJ RYAN

BOOK 1: THE NEW SCHOOL

ONE

"Wow!" Rebekah stared up at the building in front of her. "I've never gone to a school with two floors before!"

"Isn't it great?" Mouse stepped up beside her and grinned. "Just think of the water balloons we can drop from the roof!"

"Mouse!" Rebekah put her hands on her hips and turned to face her best friend. "Listen, we're starting a new school year in a brand new school. Fifth grade is going to be great—but not if you get in trouble on the first day!"

"I was just thinking about the future!"

"Make it far in the future then, please. Today is going to be perfect. I have it all mapped out." She held up a piece of paper with a map drawn on it. "I used different colors for each of my classes, so I don't even have to look at my schedule to know which way to go. With a school this big, it might be hard to get from classroom to classroom on time."

"Don't worry, I'm sure you'll make it happen!" Mouse patted her shoulder. "Alright, Magellan, ready?" He peeked in at the tiny mouse hidden in the pouch he wore around his waist.

"Oh Mouse, you shouldn't have brought him with you." Rebekah sighed. "What if he escapes?"

"I promise, I'll be very careful."

Rebekah glanced around the school grounds again.

"Oh no, Rebekah." Mouse looked at her.

"What?" Her eyes widened. "Did he already escape?"

"No, but you've got that look in your eyes."

"What look?"

"That   I'm-going-to-find-a-mystery-to-solve-before-lunch look!"

"I do not!" She laughed, then shrugged. "Well, what do you expect from me? I am Rebekah, girl detective." She patted her backpack. "I made sure I brought my detective's notebook with me, just in case."

"No surprise there." Mouse grinned, then waved at her. "See you at lunch, Rebekah, girl detective!"

As Rebekah watched Mouse run off through the open front doors of the school, her stomach flipped. This would be the first year that Mouse wouldn't be in all of her classes with her. She would know some of the other kids, but most would be brand new.

She was excited to make new friends, but she was a little nervous too.

"Alright, Rebekah." She took a deep breath, then smiled. "This is the first moment of the first best day at your new school! Let's make it count!"

As soon as she stepped through the door, a loud bell rang above her head. "Oh no!" She gasped. "I'm going to be late!"

She looked at her map, then back up to the hallways that went off in different directions. After a moment of looking around, she bolted down one of them. She ran so fast that she didn't notice someone step out in front of her until she ran right into him.

"Oof!" The man huffed as he stumbled, then landed on the floor.

"Oh no! I'm so sorry!" Rebekah jumped back and stared down at him. From his uniform she guessed that he was the janitor, and from the scowl on his face, she guessed that she was in big trouble. "I didn't see you!"

TWO

Rebekah's heart pounded as she wondered if the man was hurt.

"Do you need help getting up?" She offered her his hand.

He ignored it.

"No running!" He got to his feet and glared at her. "Do you hear me? No running in the halls!"

"Sorry, it's just that I'm late and—well, this is my first day!"

"It's everyone's first day, girly. That doesn't mean that you get to break the rules! Are you some kind of troublemaker?" The man dusted off his coveralls, then shook his head.

"No, I'm not at all! I promise!"

"I hope that turns out to be true. The first bell is just a warning. You still have two minutes to get to class." He looked up at the clock on the wall, then back at her. "Without running! If I see you do that again I will tell Principal Cooper. Understand?"

"I do." She nodded. "You're not hurt, are you?"

"I'll be fine." He grumbled as he walked off.

Rebekah started down the hall again, careful not to run. As she glanced back over her shoulder, she saw rows and rows of lockers. She didn't see a single door.

She was sure that the janitor had stepped out in front of her, but where had he come from?

"Maybe I just didn't see him?" She frowned. A glance at the clock told her she only had one minute left to get to class.

She looked back at her map and headed in a new direction. She walked as quickly as she could without technically running. A few kids shot her strange looks as she shuffled down the hall.

She reached the door for her first class and pulled it open just as the final bell rang.

"Rebekah, I presume?" A woman at the front of the class spun around to face her. She wore multiple flowers in her hair and a long flower-covered skirt.

"Yes!" Rebekah walked toward the only empty desk.

"Cutting it pretty close there. I expect my students to be here before that last bell rings. Understand?"

"Yes." Rebekah sank down in her chair and sighed. "I'm sorry, ma'am, I'll get here earlier tomorrow." She felt her cheeks grow warm. She'd planned things out so well, but so far nothing had worked out the way she'd expected.

"Ms. Bloom." The teacher pointed to the chalkboard with her name scrawled across it. It was also half-covered with several colorful flowers. "Welcome to English. Now, let's open our books and get started."

Rebekah fished her English book out of her bag. As she did, she also pulled out her detective's notebook.

Yes, she could be mistaken, but she was almost certain that the janitor had come from nowhere. Maybe her first day wasn't going so smoothly, but she already had a mystery to solve.

She couldn't help but grin at the thought of a new mystery. Rebekah was always the happiest when there was a good mystery to solve.

THREE

"I knew it." Mouse sat down beside her as she flipped her notebook open. "You already found a mystery, didn't you?"

"Maybe." Rebekah chewed on the end of her pen. "I'm not sure. But I certainly did get into trouble."

"You?" His eyes widened. "What kind of trouble?"

"I was trying to get to class on time. When I looked down at my map, the next thing I knew, I ran right into the janitor."

"Oh no. Are you okay? Is he okay?"

"Yes, I think so. But it was a pretty bad smash-up." She winced.

"So, your first mystery was finding your classroom?"

"No, that wasn't the strange part. The strange part was that I didn't see him—the janitor. The hallway was empty when I looked down at my map, and a second later, he was right in front of me." She shook her head.

"Maybe he came out of a classroom or the bathroom?"

"No, that's the thing. I looked back at the hallway and there aren't any doors in it."

"So, what are you saying?" Mouse narrowed his eyes.

"I don't know exactly. I just know that one second he wasn't there and the next he was."

"So, you think he appeared out of nowhere?" Mouse raised an eyebrow. "Do you think he was even real? Maybe he was a ghost?"

"Ghosts don't usually get knocked down when you walk into them, do they?" Rebekah frowned. "He went down pretty hard. He sure felt like a real person."

"Well, there's one way we can find out." Mouse began sorting through his tray of food.

"Mouse, what are you doing?"

"Helping you solve your mystery." Mouse grinned as he picked up his pudding cup. "Perfect!" He peeled off the top, then jumped up onto the table.

"Mouse, no!" Rebekah gasped as Mouse flung the pudding cup toward the next table full of kids.

"Food fight!" he shouted loudly.

Within seconds, pudding cups were being flung in all different directions.

Rebekah emptied her tray and used it to shield her head as a heap of mashed potatoes sailed past her and splatted Mouse right in the face.

"Oof, good one!" Mouse laughed. He jumped down off the table as teachers began to rush into the cafeteria, shouting at the students to stop.

"Mouse! How is this helpful?" Rebekah glared at him over the top of her tray.

"Just wait." Mouse grinned. Then he tipped his head toward the door.

The same man Rebekah had bumped into in the hall wheeled a mop bucket through the doors of the cafeteria and into the middle of the mess.

"Now you know he's real." Mouse smiled. "I see him too."

Suddenly the adults in the room shut all of the doors that led in and out of the cafeteria. One of them stepped to the middle of the room, almost slipping on a puddle of pudding as he did so.

"No one leaves!"

FOUR

Rebekah's heart pounded as she looked around at the giant mess, then looked back at the man in the middle of the room.

"On the first day?" The man stared at the group of kids that now sat very still. "I had hoped to introduce myself at the assembly later, but I guess this will have to be our first meeting." He put his hands on his hips. "I'm Principal Cooper—and I'm not happy."

"The principal?" Rebekah nudged Mouse with her elbow. "We're really in trouble now."

"Look at this. Would you just look at this?" Principal Cooper picked up a mashed-potato-smeared roll off the floor. "Do you know how hard Mrs. Tuttle worked to make this delicious meal for you?" He waved to a woman in a hairnet who stood near the entrance to the kitchen. "Mrs. Tuttle, have you seen what they've done?"

"Yes, Mr. Cooper." Mrs. Tuttle shook her head. "It's just terrible."

"It is." He tossed the roll from one hand to the other. "You are all going to have to be taught a lesson." He nodded to the other teachers and staff. "On the count of three."

13

Rebekah's eyes widened. "What are they going to do when they get to three?"

"I don't know!" Mouse squirmed in his seat.

"One, two..." Mr. Cooper continued to toss the roll back and forth.

The other teachers and staff began to gather up some of the food from the floor.

"Three!" Mr. Cooper shouted, then flung the roll straight at Rebekah.

"Ah!" Rebekah ducked out of the way, only to be struck by some pudding flung by Mrs. Tuttle.

The room became a commotion of thrown food and gleeful screams as all of the teachers and staff, as well as Mr. Cooper, joined in on the food fight.

Rebekah crawled underneath the table and pulled Mouse down with her. "This is crazy! What kind of principal gets in the middle of a food fight?"

"I don't know, but I love it!" Mouse laughed as he scooped up some mashed potatoes and heaved them at a passing teacher.

A few minutes later, a shrill whistle cut through all of the noise.

"That's it!" Mr. Cooper blew the whistle once more. "Play time is over. I get it, the first day of school can be a little stressful. We all make mistakes. But this is the last time I will let something like this slide, understand?" He brushed some crumbs off his tie. "Now, no one leaves this room until every table—every inch of the floor—and every wall is spotless." He nodded to the janitor. "Mr. Wiley is in charge and he will decide when you can leave. You'd all better work fast, because if you miss your next class, then you're going to have to stay after school to make up for it. Got it?"

Rebekah sighed as she began scooping up goo from the floor. "I knew it was too good to be true."

FIVE

By the time the last bell rang, Rebekah was convinced that something funny was going on at her new school. Not only was Principal Cooper strange, but she was sure that Mr. Wiley, the janitor, had appeared out of nowhere. She headed straight for the hallway where she'd bumped into him.

"I thought you might be here." Mouse walked up to her as she inspected the lockers.

"I can't shake it, Mouse. He had to have come from somewhere! But where?" She pointed to each group of lockers. "There's twelve lockers in each block and then just a small space of wall between each group. So how could he have just popped up?"

"Maybe he was hiding against the wall? Maybe the lockers blocked your view." Mouse flattened himself against the wall beside the lockers. "Go to where you were and see if you can see me."

Rebekah positioned herself at the start of the hallway, then walked forward. She noticed Mouse's shoes sticking out from the edge of the lockers right away.

"I can see you, and Mr. Wiley is much bigger than you.

Even if he was hiding, I would have seen him. Besides, why would he be hiding? Do you think he just does that? He hides and jumps out to scare kids?"

"Maybe?" Mouse shrugged. "People can be pretty weird."

"True, but I still don't think that's what happened. I would have noticed him." She sighed. "But I was busy looking at my map, so I guess maybe I could have missed him."

"Okay, let's say that he wasn't hiding. Then what is the other answer? He can walk through walls? We already know that he's real—that he's not a ghost." Mouse tapped his hand against the wall. "And this feels like a wall to me."

"Wait." Rebekah's eyes widened. "Did you hear that?"

"Hear what?" He frowned.

"Knock on the wall again." She pressed her ear up against it.

"Okay." Mouse knocked hard three times.

"Mouse!" She gasped. "The wall sounds hollow!"

"And?" Mouse shrugged. "That doesn't mean anything, does it?"

"Listen to this." Rebekah walked over to the next gap in the lockers and knocked on the wall. "See? Do you hear the difference?"

"Yes, that part of the wall isn't hollow." He frowned. "But still, he couldn't just walk through the wall, even if it is hollow."

"Unless!" Rebekah held one finger up in the air.

"Unless what?" Mouse stared at her.

"Unless it's not a wall!" Rebekah smiled. Then she began smacking the wall and kicking the lockers beside it.

"Rebekah!" Mouse rolled his eyes. "Now you're the one that's going to get us in trouble!"

SIX

Rebekah's foot hit a small button on the wall and it slid to the side.

"Wow!" Mouse jumped back as he stared at the opening. "Where did that come from?"

"It's a hidden door." Rebekah pointed to the button she'd kicked. "It's the same color as the wall, so we couldn't see it. But I noticed this." She pointed to a thin seam in the paint. "It made me think there might be something hidden here." She shivered as she looked into the dark space. "Why would there be a hidden door inside of a school?"

"I don't know, but we're going to have to find out." Mouse poked his head through the doorway, then jumped back. "Ugh, there's a terrible smell!"

"Is there?" Rebekah poked her head inside as well. It was too dark to see much, but her nose filled with an awful scent. "Yuck!" She sighed, then looked at Mouse. "But we still have to figure out where it goes."

"Why don't we let Magellan explore first?" He unzipped his pouch and looked down at the tiny mouse inside. "He can let us know what it's like inside there."

"I don't know." Rebekah frowned. "It could be dangerous."

"You don't have to worry about Magellan. He senses danger a mile away. Don't you, buddy?" Mouse smiled, then planted a kiss on the top of Magellan's head.

"I think if we're going to go in, we should all go in." Rebekah stood tall. "We just have to be careful and pay attention to where we're going."

"How can we pay attention to where we're going when we have no idea where we're going?" Mouse shook his head.

"I'm not sure exactly, but we'll figure it out." Rebekah tapped her chin. "You don't happen to have any rope with you, do you?"

"No, I didn't bring rope to school." He chuckled.

"Okay, then we'll just have to do our best." She started toward the door. As she did, she heard heavy footsteps further down the hall. "Oh no!" She peeked around the row of lockers and spotted Mr. Wiley headed straight for them.

"Mr. Wiley is going to catch us!" Rebekah gasped. "Where's that button? We have to close the door!"

"I don't know, you're the one who found it!"

"Well, I can't find it now!" She gulped as she heard the footsteps get closer.

"You there!" Mr. Wiley's voice echoed off of the lockers. "You two kids!"

"Rebekah, find that button!" Mouse zipped up Magellan's pouch.

"I'm trying!" Rebekah kicked the wall over and over. Suddenly her foot struck the button and the door slid shut. As it closed, she heard Mr. Wiley's footsteps right behind her.

"Hi, Mr. Wiley!" She spun around with a smile.

SEVEN

"What are you two doing here?" The janitor scowled at them. "School is out and there are no clubs or activities today."

"Oh, we just had so much fun today, we thought we'd stick around." Rebekah said.

"That's not how it works here." He crossed his arms. "When the final bell rings, you're supposed to leave. How am I supposed to get anything clean with the two of you tracking dirt everywhere?"

"Sorry, sir." Mouse frowned. "We didn't know."

"Well, you do now. So scat!" He pointed down the hall.

Rebekah nodded to Mouse and the two of them hurried off.

On the walk home from school, Rebekah couldn't stop thinking about Mr. Wiley.

"What if he did see us?" Rebekah frowned. "Maybe he just pretended that he didn't."

"If he saw us, then we're in big trouble."

"Maybe bigger trouble than you think." She stopped at the walkway to her house and turned to look at Mouse. "That hidden door is there for a reason. It can't be a good one."

"What do you think the reason is?" Mouse frowned.

"I'm not sure yet. But if its hidden and the students don't know about it, then my guess is it might just be for the students."

"Huh? What do you mean by that?"

"Remember how the teachers always say that next year is going to be harder?" Rebekah sighed. "I thought it was about schoolwork, but what if it's more than that? Maybe that hallway is there to give the teachers an easy way to get rid of the troublemakers."

"Oh!" Mouse's eyes widened. "Do you really think so?"

"I'm not sure why else that hidden door would be there. What do you think?"

"Maybe it's a place for the teachers to hang out and get away from the kids?"

"They have a teacher's lounge for that."

"Maybe it's there so they can play pranks on the kids?" Mouse grinned. "That would be kind of fun, wouldn't it?"

"Mouse, what kind of teachers play pranks on kids?"

"What kind of principals join in on a food fight?"

"Good point." Rebekah raised an eyebrow. "He doesn't seem like a normal principal."

"So maybe he's behind the hidden door?"

"Maybe." Rebekah shook her head. "But if you're wrong, we might be in danger."

"Danger? How?" Mouse narrowed his eyes.

"Mouse, if that secret door is there to get rid of the troublemakers, who do you think they're going to want to get rid of first? If we know about their secret door, then they might decide it would be best to get rid of us."

"What are we going to do?" Mouse gasped.

"We need to get to school early tomorrow. I'll bring supplies. We have to find out where that hallway goes before they get a chance to get rid of any of us."

"Good plan." Mouse nodded. "We'll get this figured out in no time."

"Yes, we will. Rebekah, girl detective, is on the case." She smiled.

EIGHT

Early the next morning, Rebekah pushed open the door to the school.

Although there were no other students there yet, the door was unlocked and there were cars in the parking lot.

"Do you think we can get into trouble for showing up to school too early?" Mouse winced as he followed after her.

"How can you get in trouble for wanting to be in school?" Rebekah flashed him a smile. "Don't worry, we're just going to check out the hidden door to see where it leads and then we'll blend in with the other kids when they start to arrive. We just have to make sure that we don't get caught before we get to the door."

"Great, let's do that." Mouse glanced around at the empty halls. "The teachers have to be here somewhere. There are cars outside."

"Shh!" Rebekah tugged Mouse toward the hallway with the hidden door. "They're busy doing teacher things. We'll get in and out before anyone notices."

"You're right, let's find out what's going on inside these walls!"

"It's clear." Rebekah looked both ways down the hall again. "As far as I can tell." She ran to the hidden door with Mouse on her heels. "Anyone coming now?"

"No one." Mouse peered down the hallway, then turned back to the hidden door. "Can you find the button again?"

"Should be right here." She kicked the wall hard.

The door slid open. "Here, I brought us both a flashlight." She handed one to Mouse.

"Look." Mouse unzipped Magellan's pouch and pulled the small mouse out of it. "I made sure Magellan had one too." The mouse had a tiny light held in string wrapped around his midsection.

"Wow!" Rebekah smiled. "You did a great job!"

"Thanks. I don't want him to be scared. But he might be able to help us." He set the mouse down inside the door. "He can warn us if there is anything too dangerous ahead. You're a brave little mouse, aren't you, Magellan?" He smiled as the mouse took off down the hall.

"Let's see where he goes." Rebekah ran down the hallway after him.

"It's so dusty in here—and dark!" Mouse frowned as he pointed his flashlight ahead of him. "Why would any of the teachers want to come in here?"

"Look at this." Rebekah pointed her flashlight at some tools piled against the wall. "Maybe it's still under construction. We've only seen Mr. Wiley use it."

"Do you think the other teachers don't know about it?" Mouse shined his flashlight around the hallway. "Maybe Mr. Wiley is using it to spy on them too."

"Maybe." Rebekah continued down the hall. "We'll know more when we figure out where it ends."

As she pointed the flashlight straight ahead, the sound of muffled voices filled the hallway.

"Shh!" Mouse frowned. "We must be close."

"It sounds like the teachers." Rebekah crept further down the hall. "I wonder what they're planning?"

"I doubt it's anything good." Mouse flicked his flashlight around the hallway. "This place is creepy."

"No argument there." She stopped and held up one hand. "The voices are louder now."

"What if they come in here?" Mouse took a step back.

NINE

"There." Rebekah whispered as she pointed to a sliver of light under the wall ahead of her. "It must be a door."

"There's Magellan." Mouse smiled as he spotted his pet in one of the corners.

"I think it's the teachers, but what are they saying?" Rebekah pressed her ear against the door and felt shock at what she heard.

"We're going to have to do something about the kids!"

"We have to get out of here!" Rebekah grabbed Mouse's arm. "If they figure out we're here, they're going to get rid of us right now!"

"Okay, let me just get Magellan." Mouse reached for him.

Magellan ran straight across the floor to a small opening in the wall.

"No, Magellan!" Mouse gasped, then tried to catch the tiny creature.

Before Mouse could get his hands on him, Magellan pushed through the hole into the room beyond the door.

"Oh no!" Rebekah frowned. "How are we going to get him back? Do you think they'll see him?"

High-pitched screams along with the sounds of scraping furniture carried through the wall.

"I think they've seen him." Mouse frowned.

"Get that mouse!" A woman, who sounded like Ms. Bloom, screamed.

"I have to save him!" Mouse burst through the hidden door before Rebekah could stop him.

"Don't hurt him!" Rebekah called out as she charged after Mouse.

"Well, look who we found!" Mr. Wiley put his hands on his hips as he stared right at Rebekah. "I guess I shouldn't be surprised that it's these two troublemakers."

"The mouse!" Ms. Bloom gasped from on top of a table. "Please, it's still running around!"

"Magellan!" Mouse crouched down and held out his hand to him.

The small mouse ran straight into his palm.

"Thank goodness!" Ms. Bloom sighed as she climbed down off the table.

"What are you going to do with us?" Rebekah glared at them. "Now that we know your secret, you are going to get rid of us, aren't you?"

"Aren't you a clever one?" Mr. Wiley chuckled as he looked at the teachers, then back at her. "What should we do with them? They've been very nosy and broken the rules. Would it be so bad to get rid of them?"

"Don't!" Mouse gasped. "We won't tell anyone your secret."

"Yes we will!" Rebekah huffed. "We're going to tell everyone! You can't just get rid of kids that break the rules. We all have our bad days!"

"Alright, that's enough, Mr. Wiley." Principal Cooper stepped into the room and closed the door behind him. "You've had your fun, now it's time to take care of this problem."

Rebekah's eyes widened as Principal Cooper walked straight toward her.

"Go ahead! It's not going to stop me from making sure no other kids disappear!"

"Disappear?" He laughed. "Is that what you think is going to happen to you?"

TEN

All of the teachers and Mr. Wiley began to laugh.

Rebekah glared at them. "It's not funny! It's wrong to get rid of kids!"

"No one is getting rid of anyone, Rebekah." Mr. Cooper shook his head as he held back a laugh. "You've just let your imagination run away with you."

"Is the hidden hallway something I imagined?" She crossed her arms.

"No, that's something I imagined actually." Mr. Wiley smiled. "When they designed this school, they made it so big that it's nearly impossible to get around quickly. So, I suggested we add in a corridor that would let teachers and staff get from one side of the school to the other more quickly. But it wasn't ready when the school opened. So, we had to keep it hidden for now. Once it's done, we'll have proper doors on it with keys for the staff." He shook his head. "Sorry about running into you the other day; I didn't expect anyone to be in the hall. I had to pretend it was your fault, so you wouldn't find the door."

"She found it anyway." Ms. Bloom grinned. "Such a bright girl!"

"Wait a minute." Rebekah frowned as she looked at them. "I just heard you say that you have to do something about the kids. You can pretend you aren't up to no good all you want, but I know what I heard."

"Yes, I did say that." Ms. Bloom smiled. "I said that because we do need to do something about the kids. As hard as it is for us to get to our classes, it's even harder for all of you. We've noticed that more kids are running in the hall because they are trying to get to class on time. If that keeps up someone is going to get hurt."

"Someone already did, remember?" Mr. Wiley raised an eyebrow.

"Someone else." Ms. Bloom laughed.

"That's why we've decided to expand the time between classes. We'll just trim off a few minutes of every class, to give students a bigger window to get to and from classes." Mr. Cooper looked between the two of them. "What do you think?"

"Sounds good to me." Mouse shrugged.

"Now, we should really discuss the school's pet policy." Ms. Bloom shrunk back as Mouse held Magellan up for her to see.

"Maybe we can leave that for another day." Mr. Cooper chuckled. "I think these two have been through enough already and the day is just starting."

"You really shouldn't be using that hallway, kids." Mr. Wiley shook his head. "It's still being built and not even the teachers are using it yet. Can you promise me you'll stay out of it?"

"We promise." Rebekah nodded. She was glad that the mystery was solved and even more glad that her teachers had no intention of getting rid of her or any other students. "I think more time is a great idea."

"I hope that means you'll make it to my class on time, Rebekah?" Ms. Bloom smiled.

"I will, Ms. Bloom, I promise."

Mr. Cooper opened the door to the teacher's lounge. "All of the other students are arriving. You two should get ready for class."

Rebekah walked toward the door with Mouse behind her.

Once outside, Mr. Cooper closed the door behind him.

"Can you believe they just let us go?" Rebekah smiled. "No detention or anything!"

"That's a relief." Mouse sighed. "I guess there isn't a big mystery at our new school after all."

"I don't know." Rebekah looked over her shoulder at the teacher's lounge. "I'd say Principal Cooper is a pretty big mystery. He's always saying and doing things that surprise me." She took her backpack off and pulled her notebook out as Mouse shook his head at her.

"What?" She grinned as she started to write. "Just noting a few clues."

"I'd expect nothing less." Mouse smiled back at her.

And just like that, an exciting new school year had begun for Rebekah, girl detective.

BOOK 2: THE SCIENCE TEACHER

ONE

"So, what's your favorite part about being at a new school this year, Mouse?" Rebekah smiled as she popped a chicken nugget into her mouth.

"I'd say it's the sports fields—especially the baseball field. It's great!" He chomped down on a chicken nugget as well.

"Yeah, they are great. I tried out the soccer field yesterday and the grass is so nice and there are new goals. It's really awesome!" She took a sip of her water. "But I think what I like best are the science labs. There's so much equipment! I can't wait to use the microscopes. Mr. Bromley, the science teacher, is really nice too."

"There are lots of great things about this new school, but this healthy food kick is a little annoying." Mouse poked at the carrots on his plate.

"They're good for you." Rebekah grinned. "Just eat one, you might like it."

"It's orange." He sighed. "Food shouldn't be orange."

"What about pumpkin pie?" She laughed.

"Pumpkin pie is the only exception." He nodded. "Now, if

they gave me pumpkin pie instead of carrots, I'd definitely eat it."

"Mouse! That wouldn't be healthy."

"Why not? Pumpkins are vegetables, aren't they?" He smiled.

"Well, it depends on who you ask. Botanists may consider it a fruit!"

"Great, is there anything you don't know?" Mouse rolled his eyes.

"Well, I do know that pumpkin pie is a dessert!" She laughed. "Just eat your carrot, Mouse!"

"Not a chance." He picked up his tray and carried it over to the cart to return to the kitchen. As he walked away from it, someone walked right up behind him.

"What's Mr. Bromley doing with your tray?" Rebekah watched as her science teacher picked up Mouse's plate. "Maybe he's going to try to make you eat your vegetables?"

"Right, if my mom can't get me to do it, there is no chance that Mr. Bromley will."

"What is he doing?" Rebekah gasped as she watched him grab Mouse's carrots off of the plate and slip them into his pocket.

"He's stealing my carrots." Mouse raised an eyebrow. "I guess technically they're not mine anymore, since I wasn't going to eat them. Is that still stealing?"

"Mouse! That's not the point." Rebekah frowned. "The point is why is he taking them?"

"Uh-oh, here it comes." Mouse grinned. "I see that look in your eyes."

"I do think it's important for us to find out what's going on here. It's not normal for teachers to steal leftover vegetables, is it?" She dug into her backpack and pulled out her detective's notebook. "It may be a small mystery, but some do start out small. Let's see where it takes us."

She flipped open her notebook and began writing down the details of Mr. Bromley's theft.

"I'll leave it to Rebekah, girl detective, to figure out. I don't ever want to see those carrots again!" Mouse grinned.

TWO

Rebekah sat down at her desk in science class and stared at her teacher. Mr. Bromley sat in his chair behind his desk and stared at his computer.

The other kids in the class wandered the room to check out the different equipment that had been set up.

"Careful, kids!" Mr. Bromley looked up from his computer. "All of the equipment is very expensive. If we break any of it, we may not be able to replace it."

Rebekah watched as he stood up. Were the carrots still in his pocket? She scrunched up her nose at the thought.

"Alright, let's get started. Today we can learn about the different parts of the microscope and how we're going to use them. So right now, I need to see all of your hands in the air. Got it?" He walked around his desk over to the other students. "Let's go, Rebekah, don't you want to try out one of the microscopes?"

Rebekah jumped to her feet. "Absolutely!"

Maybe it was odd that Mr. Bromley had hidden carrots in his pocket, but that didn't make him a bad teacher.

He showed all of the students how to use the microscopes.

"A gentle touch is very important. A nudge or a knock could

really mess up your focus. So here in our lab, we'll need to have quiet feet and gentle hands, okay?"

"I can do that." Rebekah smiled as he walked up to her.

"Great, Rebekah. I thought you could. Show me how you switch your magnification." He smiled as he watched her adjust the microscope. "Very good, Rebekah."

"Hey, Mr. Bromley, what's your favorite vegetable?"

"Rebekah, I'm not sure what that has to do with microscopes." He frowned.

"I'm just curious." She smiled. "I really love carrots. Don't you?"

"Actually, no." He shrugged. "I'm not very fond of carrots. They're a little too orange for me."

"Exactly!" Mouse called out from behind his microscope.

Rebekah stared at Mr. Bromley as questions flooded her mind. If he didn't like carrots, why had he taken Mouse's? Why had he put them in his pocket?

"Now, I can't stress enough how important it is to be very careful with this equipment." Mr. Bromley began to walk around the classroom as he spoke.

Rebekah didn't know much about her teacher, but now she knew that he had something to hide. Why steal the carrots and then lie about it?

She looked across the classroom at Mouse.

Mouse looked up at her and raised his eyebrows.

Yes, the mystery had to be solved, even if that meant digging a little bit more into her teacher's vegetable stealing ways.

"Rebekah!" Mr. Bromley sighed as he walked over to her. "You're leaning on the slides! What are you thinking?"

"Oh, sorry, Mr. Bromley." Rebekah stepped back. "I didn't see them there."

He looked straight into her eyes. His brows knit with frustration. "Rebekah, you need to be more careful. Understand?"

THREE

"Yes, sir." Rebekah's heart pounded. "I'll be more careful, I promise."

"Good." Mr. Bromley stared at her a moment longer, then turned to the rest of the class. "That's all for today. We're going to carefully pack up our supplies. Tomorrow, we'll have a chance to look at some new ones."

As the other kids filed out of the classroom, Mouse walked over to Rebekah.

"That was weird, huh?"

Mr. Bromley walked back to his desk.

"Very." Rebekah sighed. "Why would he take the carrots if he doesn't like carrots?"

"Maybe he just threw them out." Mouse shrugged.

Rebekah looked over at Mr Bromley where he sat behind his desk. She watched as he slipped his hand into his pocket and pulled out a handful of carrots. Her eyes widened as he dropped them into one of the desk drawers.

She jumped at the sound of the drawer sliding shut. When she looked up again, Mr. Bromley was staring straight at her.

"What are you two still doing here? Don't you have another class to get to?"

Rebekah gulped, grabbed her backpack, and headed for the door.

Mouse followed right after her.

Once in the hall, Mouse grabbed her arm. "Rebekah, I think he knows we saw him."

"I do too." She looked over her shoulder toward the classroom. "And he didn't look happy about it."

"It's no big deal, right?" Mouse shrugged. "They're just vegetables. It's not like he's stealing anything that anybody wants."

"Some people do like vegetables, Mouse." She huffed. "But that's not the point. The point is that he's hiding something and we need to find out what it is. I'm afraid that he's already not too happy with me. So, we'll have to be careful."

"Just like he told you." Mouse raised an eyebrow. "To be more careful."

"Yes." Rebekah frowned. "I wonder if he was talking about the slides or me spying on him."

"I'm sure it was about the slides. What we need to figure out is why he is stealing the vegetables."

"If we knew that, there wouldn't be a mystery to solve." Rebekah laughed.

"You're right. What I mean is, why would he steal the vegetables? What reason could he have?"

"Well, he is the science teacher. Maybe he plans on doing an experiment with them? But why would he hide it?" She shook her head.

"Maybe he wants to surprise us?" Mouse winced. "Although, I'm not sure what kind of science experiment he could do with vegetables. I'm not sure I want to know either."

"Maybe he's just hungry." Rebekah's heart dropped. "Oh,

what if it's that he doesn't have enough food to eat at home, so he has to take the leftover vegetables?"

"That would be terrible." Mouse rubbed his stomach. "I'm not sure I'd ever be hungry enough to want vegetables, but if he is, that's not good at all. My mom does say that teachers don't make enough money. She's always buying supplies for the school, because she says many teachers buy things with their own money."

"Then it is possible." Rebekah sighed. "If he is stealing old vegetables, he must be starving!"

FOUR

Rebekah spent the rest of the day thinking about Mr. Bromley's situation.

She had learned quite a bit about people who didn't have enough food during the Christmas food drive she'd helped out with. She'd gone door to door in her neighborhood with her mother and filled bags full of donated food. She decided the best way to help Mr. Bromley was to do the same thing.

During art class, she grabbed a few pieces of poster board and a big box. She printed in big letters on the poster board: *Food Drive Help The Hungry.*

Then she cut out pictures of food from magazines and decorated the box with them.

"Rebekah, what are you creating?" Her art teacher smiled as she looked at the box.

"I want to have a food drive. So, I'm making posters and a collection box."

"Great job." She patted Rebekah's shoulder. "It's always wonderful to want to help others."

Rebekah thought about Mr. Bromley coming to school

hungry. She just hoped the signs would be enough to get the other students to bring in food to donate.

As she carried the box out of the classroom, her teacher stopped her.

"Wait a minute, Rebekah." She reached into her desk drawer and pulled out a box of crackers. "It's not much, but it will get you started." She dropped the crackers into Rebekah's donation box.

"Thanks so much, Mrs. Carlisle! I'm sure he will love it." She smiled.

"He?" Mrs. Carlisle raised an eyebrow. "Is this collection just for one person? Or for the local food pantry?"

"Uh, it's going to a very good cause." Rebekah flashed her another smile then hurried out into the hall. She didn't want to embarrass Mr. Bromley by telling another teacher how hungry he was.

"Mouse! Look what I made!" Rebekah showed him the box. "It's to collect food for Mr. Bromley!"

"It looks great!" He reached into the box. "My favorite crackers!"

"Not for you!" Rebekah smacked his hand away. "You're not hungry."

"I'm always hungry!" Mouse groaned. "But you're right. Mr. Bromley should have them. Do you want me to help you put up those signs?"

"That would be great, thanks!"

Rebekah and Mouse put a sign up near the front door and another one near the cafeteria.

"Let's put the box right outside Mr. Bromley's classroom. That way if it gets too heavy, we won't have far to carry it."

"Good thinking." Mouse followed her to the room. The last bell had already rung for the day and most of the kids had left or were at their clubs or sports practices.

Rebekah expected Mr. Bromley's classroom to be empty too. She put the box right next to his door.

"There, I bet by tomorrow afternoon it will be full!"

"What's this?" Mr. Bromley poked his head out through the door. "What are you up to now, Rebekah?"

FIVE

Rebekah's heart pounded. She wasn't sure what to expect. Would Mr. Bromley be angry that she'd set the donation box outside his door?

"Oh, nothing really Mr. Bromley." Rebekah stepped in front of the box.

"Nothing?" He raised an eyebrow. "It sure looks like something."

"I'm just taking up a collection." Rebekah smiled. "A food collection—for people who might be hungry."

"Ah." He nodded, then smiled. "Very nice idea, Rebekah. Continue on." He turned and walked down the hall.

"He didn't take the crackers." Mouse frowned.

"Of course he's not going to take the crackers. He doesn't know that it's for him. But by tomorrow, he'll be in for a great surprise!" Rebekah headed toward the door. "Let's hit some houses on the way home. Maybe people will have some extra food to donate to the cause."

"Sounds good." Mouse followed after her.

At each house they came to, Rebekah knocked and Mouse held his backpack open.

"Hi, we're collecting food for our hungry teacher." Rebekah smiled at the woman who lived next door to her. The family was new to the neighborhood and she had yet to meet them.

"Your hungry teacher?" She frowned. "He doesn't have any food?"

"No, and he's so hungry that he's eating vegetables!" Mouse winced.

"What does this town pay its teachers?" She shook her head. "None of them should be hungry. Hold on, I just went to the store. I have plenty I can give."

"Great!" Rebekah grinned.

A few minutes later, Mouse limped towards Rebekah's door with his backpack gripped in both hands. "I think that last house put us over the top. This bag is heavy!"

"It's wonderful, isn't it?" Rebekah took the bag from him. "Mr. Bromley will be so surprised."

"And full." Mouse nodded.

"I'll see you in the morning, Mouse." Rebekah waved to him, then stepped inside.

She imagined what Mr. Bromley would say upon seeing the full box of food and finding out that it was for him.

Oh Rebekah, what a kind thing to do!

It was nothing, Mr. Bromley. Eat up!

"It'll be perfect." Rebekah smiled as she continued to imagine the next day.

She sat down on the edge of her bed and flipped her detective's notebook open. As she read over the notes she had made, she frowned. "I guess this mystery has been solved." She stared down at the words on the paper. "Unless..." Her eyes widened. "Unless he's not really hungry at all."

The thought made her mind race. What else could be causing Mr. Bromley to collect unwanted vegetables? It was the only thing that made sense. She was sure that Mr. Bromley would be thrilled to have so much food to take home with him.

"I guess I'll find out tomorrow." She sighed and flipped the notebook shut. Now she just had to find a way to be patient.

SIX

Early the next morning, Rebekah and Mouse hauled bags of food into the school. When they reached Mr. Bromley's classroom, the door was still locked.

"Good, we beat him here. Let's just drop the food off, and then during class, we can present him with it." She smiled. "He's going to be so excited!"

"I sure hope so." Mouse rubbed his shoulder as he set his backpack on the floor.

Rebekah started tossing food into the box, then stepped back to let Mouse do the same.

"Good morning, Rebekah. And Mouse, is it?" Mr. Cooper, the principal, walked up to them.

"Good morning Mr. Cooper." Rebekah looked up. She still wasn't sure what to think of him. He had some very strange habits for a principal.

"It's Mouse, yes." Mouse pushed his hair back from his eyes. "Good morning, Mr. Cooper."

"I see you two are filling that box up." He nodded. "Good job." His eyes narrowed. "What food pantry will you be donating it to?"

"Uh, it's a special drive—for one person." Rebekah glanced at Mouse. "We're hoping to fill up his entire kitchen."

"Great." The principal stared at Rebekah a moment longer, then turned his attention to Mouse. "This wouldn't be some kind of prank, would it, Mouse?"

"Prank?" Mouse squeaked. "Me?"

"I have read a bit about your activities at your old school. I just hope you know that things are different at my school."

"Sure." Mouse gulped.

"Don't worry, Mr. Cooper, this isn't any prank. Just our way of helping." Rebekah spotted Mr. Bromley as he walked down the hallway. "Anyway, we'd better get to class. We don't want to be late. Right, Mouse?"

"Right." Mouse hurried past her in the direction of his first class.

Rebekah walked off in the opposite direction.

As she passed Mr. Bromley, she noticed that he had a container tucked under his arm. It appeared to be full of salad. She frowned as she wondered what dumpster he might have pulled it out of just to make sure he had something to eat. Soon, he wouldn't have to think twice about where he'd get his next meal.

Rebekah was excited about getting to science class that afternoon. But at lunch, she decided to check on Mr. Bromley. She wanted to make sure he was eating something good.

When she neared his classroom, she noticed his door was open. She spotted him inside with his container of salad. It didn't look too fresh, but it also didn't look like it was picked out of the garbage. As she watched, he slipped a piece of lettuce into his bottom desk drawer. He snapped it shut, then looked up.

"Rebekah, what are you doing out in the hall? Aren't you supposed to be at lunch?"

"Yes, I am. I'm on my way." She frowned. He couldn't even eat his entire lunch without saving some for dinner. She was tempted to tell him the box of food was for him, but she didn't want to take all of the credit. "See you in class, Mr. Bromley." She waved to him, then hurried down the hall.

SEVEN

Later that day, Rebekah walked into Mr. Bromley's class. It felt more like she was floating, actually. Her heart pounded with excitement.

She smiled at Mr. Bromley as she walked past him.

"What's going on out there?" Mr. Bromley stood up and walked over to one of the windows that overlooked the front of the school.

Rebekah looked out the window too. A group of people had gathered together and were marching back and forth in front of the school. Some of them held signs, but Rebekah couldn't read what the signs said.

"It looks like some kind of protest." Rebekah frowned. "Maybe they don't like how noisy the bell is."

"Maybe." Mr. Bromley shook his head. He smiled at the other students that filed into the classroom. "Alright, everyone, let's get started."

"Actually, Mr. Bromley?" Rebekah raised her hand.

"Yes Rebekah?"

"I have a special presentation I'd like to make—if that's okay." She stood up from her desk.

"A special presentation? I didn't assign any presentations. Did I?" He began to flip through a notebook on the desk in front of him.

"No, you didn't assign this." Rebekah glanced over at Mouse and then at the other students before she looked back at Mr. Bromley. "We wanted to do something special for you. Since you're such a great teacher."

"Something special?" He sat back in his chair, his eyes wide. Then he smiled. "Well, that's very kind of you, Rebekah. I suppose we can spare a few moments for your presentation. But I must say, I'm not sure what I did to earn such kindness."

"Listen, Mr. Bromley, you come here every day to make sure our minds are filled with knowledge. We want to make sure that you come here every day with a full belly." She waved to Mouse.

Mouse followed her out the door to the large donation box.

Rebekah pulled it hard.

Mouse gave it a shove.

The box barely moved.

"We might need a little help." Rebekah winced as she pulled again.

"Rebekah, what is this all about?" Mr. Bromley walked to the door. "Why are you bringing that box in here?"

"Because it's for you, Mr. Bromley." She smiled at him. "I think it will fill up your kitchen very nicely, don't you?"

"I'm sure it would." He shook his head. "But I don't understand. Why are you giving all this food to me?"

"Attention students!" Mr. Cooper's voice barked over the speaker in the classroom. "Due to a protest on school grounds, we are going to have early dismissal today. Everyone gather your things."

A few of the students—including Mouse—cheered as they picked up their backpacks.

"Just take it home with you, Mr. Bromley." Rebekah looked into his eyes. "So you won't have to be hungry anymore."

"Rebekah." He sighed.

"Bye!" She grabbed her backpack and ran for the hall.

She and Mouse walked past the group of people who continued to march in front of the school.

"I think he was a little embarrassed. But now at least he'll have food." Rebekah smiled.

EIGHT

As Rebekah and Mouse walked home from school, she noticed Mr. Bromley's car not far ahead of her. She saw it turn into the local food pantry.

"What is he doing?" Rebekah frowned.

"Maybe he's still hungry?" Mouse shrugged.

Mr. Bromley backed his car up to the door and popped open his trunk. He spoke with one of the employees, then the two of them lifted the large box out of the trunk of his car.

"He's donating it?" Rebekah gasped. "Why would he do that? We worked so hard to make sure he had plenty to eat."

"Maybe he's a picky eater?" Mouse shook his head. "It's hard to believe, since he seems to like vegetables."

"Something is not right here." Rebekah crossed her arms. "I am going to find out what is going on!"

"Okay, but can we do that tomorrow?" Mouse rubbed his stomach. "All this talk about food is making me really hungry for my afternoon snack."

"Yes, tomorrow." Rebekah frowned as she watched Mr. Bromley drive away from the food pantry. It didn't make any sense for him to give away food if he was hungry—which meant he might not be hungry after all.

Rebekah spent the rest of the night going over her notes in her detective's notebook. She added a few more about his reaction to the food and how he dropped it off at the food pantry.

The next morning, as she walked to school with Mouse, she shook her head. "I think Mr. Bromley is up to something. I don't think he's hungry at all. He might even be keeping those vegetables for another reason."

"What if he plans to make us eat them?" Mouse winced. "If you forget your homework, you have to eat a piece of broccoli. If you don't raise your hand to ask a question, that'll be a handful of corn!"

"That seems a little crazy, doesn't it, Mouse?" Rebekah sighed as they approached the school.

"Is it crazier than hiding vegetables in your desk?" Mouse shrugged.

"You're right. We need to see inside that drawer. I bet there will be a clue inside that will tell us what he's up to. But how are we going to get into it?"

"Oh, don't worry, I'm sure I can help you with that." Mouse grinned.

"I don't know who told you what, but you have bad information!" Mr. Cooper stood in front of the school with his hands on his hips as he spoke to the protesters that had already gathered. "Our teachers are paid more than enough to eat! Not a single one of them is hungry, and if they were, I would make sure they had plenty to eat myself! Now please, stop this!"

Rebekah winced as she glanced at Mouse. "Uh-oh."

"Uh-oh is right. If Mr. Cooper finds out that it was us that told people around town that the teachers don't have enough to eat, he's not going to be happy."

"We have to get inside that drawer." Rebekah looked straight at Mouse. "I've noticed that he keeps it open most of the time and only pushes it closed when someone walks toward him. If you can distract him, I might be able to get a peek inside."

"Okay, I can do that." Mouse patted the pouch he wore around his waist. "I know a little guy who is great at distracting people."

"Hi, everyone." Mr. Bromley sat down on the front of his desk and looked at the students. "I want to thank you all for being so kind to me yesterday. But I think it's important that you understand that I have plenty of money for food. I eat three healthy meals a day. So please don't think that you need to donate food to me. However, if you do have extra food you'd like to give away, there is a great food pantry right here in our town that would happily accept your donations."

Rebekah sank down in her chair. She'd only wanted to solve a mystery, and instead, she'd started a protest.

She watched as Mr. Bromley walked behind his desk. He glanced down at the bottom drawer of the desk, smiled, then turned to the chalkboard. "Alright, now that we've settled that, let's talk a little bit about the slides we're going to take a look at today." He picked up a piece of chalk and began to draw on the chalkboard.

Rebekah looked over at Mouse.

Mouse gave her a short nod, then he unzipped the pouch he wore around his waist. He pulled out his pet mouse, Magellan, and looked into his eyes. Then he set the mouse down on the floor beside his desk.

Rebekah waited for the first scream.

It came from the boy who sat beside her. He screamed and jumped up onto his chair.

"Mouse!"

"What?" Mouse smiled.

"No, not you, Mouse!" The boy rolled his eyes. "A real mouse!" He pointed at the floor.

Several more screams followed. A few people jumped up on their chairs, but more rushed for the door.

"What's going on here?" Mr. Bromley spun around to face them. "Everyone sit down! Don't push! Watch out for the equipment!"

He ran around the front of his desk. "Class is not over!"

"Watch out, Mr. Bromley, it's headed straight for you!" a girl called out from the back of the classroom.

"Mouse!" Mr. Bromley gasped as the tiny creature ran toward him.

"What?" Mouse smiled again. "I'm not doing anything!"

"Get it!" someone shouted from the front of the room.

"No, just run!" another student gasped and bolted for the door.

As the rest of the students ran out into the hall, Rebekah rushed behind the desk. She pulled the drawer open and looked inside.

"Hay?" She looked up at Mouse. "He's eating hay?"

Mouse scooped Magellan up, then peered into the drawer. "I see some carrots in there too."

"Is that mouse poop?" Rebekah gasped.

"It's too big to be mouse poop."

"What are you doing?" Mr. Bromley stood in the doorway of the classroom.

TEN

"What have *you* been doing Mr. Bromley?" Rebekah put her hands on her hips as she turned to face him. "Why are you stealing vegetables? Why are you eating hay? What has been pooping in your drawer?"

Before Mr. Bromley could answer, his suit jacket wiggled.

"Uh..." Mouse stared at him.

"Be still," Mr. Bromley hissed at his suit jacket.

It wiggled again and a bit of fluff poked out from the hem of it.

"What is that?" Rebekah's eyes widened.

"Just what is going on in here?" Mr. Cooper's voice boomed from the hallway before he even stepped into the classroom. "Why are students screaming in the hallway? Mr. Bromley?" He narrowed his eyes. "What is sticking out of your jacket?"

"Okay, I can explain everything." Mr. Bromley sighed. He reached into his suit jacket and pulled out a small brown bunny with a fluffy white tail. "This is Chompers and he gets very hungry."

"Chompers?" Rebekah stared at the bunny. "You've been stealing vegetables to feed your rabbit?"

"I don't steal them." He sighed. "I just grab some of what is left behind at lunch. It keeps him happy during the day."

"Why exactly do you have a rabbit in your classroom?" Mr. Cooper crossed his arms.

"Last year, at the old school, Chompers was our class pet. I know this new school has a no pets policy, but I just couldn't stand to leave Chompers at home all day. So, I brought him to school with me. I figured if I kept him safe and sound in my drawer, he wouldn't cause any harm. I take him out to let him run around on my breaks and at lunch. I know it's not the best situation, but he gets so lonely at home."

"Mr. Bromley, give me the rabbit." Mr. Cooper held out his hands.

"What? No. I'll just take him home."

"Give him to me now." Mr. Cooper frowned. "You violated school policy. We all have to follow the rules."

Mouse gulped and folded his hands over the pouch he'd tucked Magellan into.

"Please, Mr. Cooper, this is all my fault." Rebekah stepped forward. "Let Mr. Bromley keep his rabbit."

"Give me Chompers." Mr. Cooper took the rabbit. "I'm going to find him a new home."

"Mr. Cooper, you can't!" Rebekah gasped.

Without another word, Mr. Cooper turned and walked away.

REBEKAH COULDN'T SLEEP that night. She had solved the mystery, but it had only made things much worse. She woke up the next morning, determined to get Chompers back for Mr. Bromley.

When she and Mouse arrived at school, she marched

straight toward the principal's office. Before she could reach it, she heard Mouse gasp.

"Rebekah! Look at this!" He pointed to something new along the wall just outside the principal's office.

"It's a hutch!" Rebekah grinned as she looked over the large wooden structure. It had plenty of room for Chompers to run in and large plastic windows that they could look through.

"This is fantastic!" Mouse grinned.

"Mr. Bromley will be so happy. Now we can all enjoy seeing Chompers every day!"

"Yes, and Chompers can enjoy my carrots every day too!" Mouse laughed.

As the principal's door opened, Rebekah froze.

Mr. Cooper looked straight at her. He didn't smile. He didn't speak. He just closed the door again.

Rebekah was glad Chompers had a new home, but she still wasn't any closer to solving another mystery.

Just what kind of principal was Mr. Cooper?

BOOK 3: GIRL IN THE WINDOW

ONE

"This place looks amazing!" Rebekah stepped off of the school bus. "It's like going back in time!"

"I can't wait to churn some butter!" Mouse grinned as he stepped off the bus behind her. "It looks like so much fun."

"Alright, kids—everyone, gather together and listen up!" Mr. Cooper, the principal, waved until he had all of their attention. "Today's field trip is meant to give you a taste of what it was like to live a long time ago. They didn't have all of the fancy things that we do now. So, I'd like each of you to drop your devices, phones, tablets, smartwatches, and whatever gadgets you have in this bag." He held out a bag. "You'll get them back at the end of the day."

"Sure thing." Mouse walked up to him and dropped his phone into the bag.

"What do you have in there?" Mr. Cooper pointed to the pouch Mouse wore around his waist. "Any devices?"

"No, nothing electronic." Mouse took a step back.

"Open it up. Let me see." Mr. Cooper narrowed his eyes.

"Mr. Cooper!" Rebekah dropped her phone into the bag he held. "I can't wait to get to the tour! Where do we start? I'm so excited! Can you tell me a little bit about what happened here, or do we have to wait for the tour guide?"

While Rebekah distracted the principal, Mouse disappeared into the crowd of kids.

"Rebekah, you'll have to wait for the guide just like everyone else." Mr Cooper frowned as he looked past her. "Now where did Mouse go?"

"I'll find him!" Rebekah smiled, then disappeared into the crowd as well. When she caught up with Mouse, she grinned. "That was close, huh? Is Magellan okay?"

"A little spooked, I think." Mouse frowned. "Mr. Cooper sure is getting nosy. Do you think he knows that you've got an open case in your detective's notebook about him?"

"I hope not." Rebekah adjusted her backpack on her shoulders. "I'm sure he wouldn't be too happy about it. But let's not worry about that today. We're here to have some fun. We'll just have to do our best to stay out of his way."

"I'm not the one investigating him, am I?" Mouse raised his eyebrows.

"You have to admit, he is a bit strange." Rebekah shook her head, then grabbed Mouse's arm. "Hurry! The tour is starting."

"This village was once fully operational. There were a few stores and homes, as well as a large working farm. So today, you will all get a chance to see what life was like long ago." The tour guide—who wore an old-fashioned dress—pointed to the different buildings. "You can explore any of the buildings except for that house on the end. That one is closed for repairs."

Rebekah looked at the house that the guide pointed to. It had two levels and small attic windows at the top. She tried to imagine what it would be like to live in that house.

As she stared at the window, a girl waved to her from behind the glass.

TWO

Shocked, Rebekah blinked. Had she really seen what she thought she'd seen?

She glanced around at the other students. Were any missing? She'd only caught a glimpse of the girl, but she didn't recognize her.

She looked back up at the window and saw the girl wave again.

Rebekah raised her hand to wave back to her.

"Who are you waving to?" Mouse looked at her with a funny expression.

"The girl—in the window." She glanced at him, then looked back at the window. The sun reflected off the glass. She squinted, but she couldn't see the girl anymore.

"What girl?" Mouse frowned. "That house is empty. Didn't you hear the tour guide? It's closed for repairs."

"I know I saw her." Rebekah crossed her arms. "She waved to me and I waved back."

"I'm sorry, but I don't see anyone there now." He shrugged. "Maybe it was your imagination? Or a reflection of something?"

"I know what I saw, Mouse." Rebekah squinted up at the

window again. She still couldn't make anyone out. "Let's take a closer look. Then you'll be able to see her too."

"I don't know if that's a good idea. We're not supposed to go anywhere near that house." Mouse glanced over at Mr. Cooper. "I don't think I should do anything to draw Mr. Cooper's attention to me. If he finds out I have Magellan with me, he's not going to be happy."

"I know. We won't go inside. We'll just get a little closer, so that the sun isn't blinding us. I'm telling you, Mouse, I saw her in there. If the house is off limits, then what is a girl doing inside of it? We have to find out." She slipped her backpack off her shoulders.

"Rebekah, this isn't a mystery." Mouse raised an eyebrow as she pulled out her detective's notebook. "It's just a trick of the light. Like you said, no one is allowed in there."

"Maybe you're right, but I have to find out either way." She jotted down a few notes in her notebook. "Otherwise, I'll be thinking about it the whole day."

"Alright, fine. Let's do it." Mouse looked over at Mr. Cooper. "Mr. Cooper is going off with one of the groups. We should be safe to sneak over."

"Great! Let's go." Rebekah tucked her notebook under her arm and picked up her backpack.

As they walked toward the house, she peered up at the window again. She caught a glimpse of a hand pressed against the window.

"Mouse! Do you see that!" She grabbed his arm and pointed.

THREE

"What?" Mouse looked up at the window. He shielded his eyes with one hand. "I don't see anything!"

"There was a hand pressed against the window!" Rebekah sighed. "But it's gone now. She must have given up on us seeing her. Now the sun is back too." She squinted, then shook her head. "It's impossible for us to see from out here."

"If we go into that house, we could get into big trouble." Mouse frowned. "I'm not saying I won't go, but you should know that Mr. Cooper is not going to be happy if he catches us."

"I know that." Rebekah looked up at the window again. "But how can I just ignore her? She was trying to get my attention. I know she was."

"Okay, let's think about this. Let's say that there is a girl in the house. Why would she be in there?"

"Maybe she wanted to check it out?" Rebekah shrugged. "It's kind of cool—in a creepy sort of way."

"But she's not supposed to be in there. Which means she's breaking the rules. Why would she want us to see her if she's breaking the rules?" His eyes widened. "Oh no!"

"What?" She looked up at the window. "Did you see her?"

"No. But I just thought of something."

"What is it?"

"This is a super old house, right?" He touched the old wooden railing that led up onto the porch.

"Yes. So what?"

"So maybe the girl you're seeing in the window isn't a girl at all!" He leaned closer to her. "Maybe she's a ghost!"

"A ghost?" Rebekah laughed. "I saw her, Mouse. She was real, just like you and me."

"Ghosts can look real. They're not all see-through and spooky. Most of the ghost stories I've heard start with a really old house. That might explain why you saw her and I didn't. Maybe she only wants your attention." He looked up at the window. "But if she is a ghost, we have to be careful. Ghosts can be pretty tricky."

"I don't think she's a ghost, Mouse. I think you didn't see her because the sun was hitting the window. But you're right, I've heard a lot of ghost stories involving old houses too. Even if she is a ghost, we have to find out for sure what's going on in there." Rebekah opened her notebook and wrote down a few more notes. "Don't ghosts usually come out at night?"

"You're thinking of vampires." Mouse bent down to tie his shoe. "Ghosts can come out any time—day or night." As he stood back up, the zipper on the pouch around his waist caught on his belt loop and pulled open. Magellan jumped right out.

"Mouse!" Rebekah gasped. "Magellan!"

FOUR

"No! No! Magellan!" Mouse lunged for his pet, but Magellan bolted away from him and through a small crack in the corner of the house. "Come back here!" Mouse groaned.

"I guess we'll just have to go inside and find him." Rebekah shrugged. "Nothing we can do about it now."

"We have no choice!" Mouse sighed, then looked over his shoulder. "Everyone seems pretty distracted. We should be able to get inside without being caught."

"Great, let's go." Rebekah slid her notebook into her backpack, then started up the creaky stairs to the front door of the house.

"Magellan!" Mouse peered through one of the windows on the porch. "I see him! He just ran into the kitchen!"

"The door is unlocked." Rebekah pushed it open. It creaked almost as loudly as the stairs did. "Hurry, Mouse, before someone sees us."

Mouse ran through the door and right into the kitchen.

While Mouse searched for Magellan, Rebekah took a look around the house. She noticed that there were several stacks of wood, a drill, and a ladder pushed off to one side.

"I guess this place really is closed for repairs. Maybe it's not haunted after all. But I know what I saw." She followed Mouse into the kitchen. "Did you catch him yet?"

"No! He's playing games with me!" Mouse frowned as Magellan ran right through his hands.

"Let me help." Rebekah crouched down and held her hands out. "Scare him this way and I'll catch him."

"He's too smart for that." Mouse shook his head. "But I'll try." He crept up to the mouse and gave his bottom a light tap.

Magellan squeaked, then ran straight toward Rebekah.

"That's right, Magellan. Come right to me." She crouched down even further, ready to pounce. She felt his soft coat as he ran into her hands. Then she felt his tiny feet as he pushed right through them and ran back out into the living room area.

"Rebekah! Grab him!"

"He's too fast!" Rebekah frowned. "I'm sorry, he got away again!"

"Alright, we'll have to trap him." Mouse grabbed a bucket from the kitchen and carried it into the living room.

Magellan stopped at the bottom of the stairs and peered up at Mouse.

"Look at him, he's just waiting for me to try to catch him! Magellan, you're a naughty mouse!"

"Get him!" Rebekah ran toward Mouse and Magellan.

"Don't, you'll scare him off!" Mouse lunged toward Magellan.

Magellan squeaked, but couldn't escape Mouse's grasp.

"Got you!" Mouse grinned as he scooped Magellan up. "You shouldn't scare me like that, Magellan!" He tucked the mouse back into his pouch and zipped it closed. "Now, we should get out of here before we get caught."

"What about the girl?" Rebekah frowned.

"We don't even know if there is a girl! But we do know that Principal Cooper is out there, and if we don't show up soon, he's going to be looking for us."

A loud thump above their heads made them both freeze.

FIVE

"Something is up there." Rebekah whispered. "We have to see what it is."

"You're right, there really is a mystery here." Mouse met her eyes. "Let's figure it out!"

"Up the stairs." Rebekah pointed and then climbed up the steps with Mouse right behind her. Once they reached the landing of the second floor, she put her finger to her lips. "Listen; maybe she will make another sound."

Mouse nodded, then stood very still.

Rebekah listened as hard as she could. She heard some creaks from the house. She also heard Magellan scratching inside Mouse's pouch. She even heard the tour guide not far off explaining the history of the village. But she didn't hear any more thumps.

"Hello?" She looked down the hallway. "Is someone here?"

"Someone alive?" Mouse called out.

"Mouse!" Rebekah frowned.

"What? I think it's a valid question."

"If you were a ghost, would you want someone to ask you that?" She sighed.

"Maybe?" He shrugged. "I've never been a ghost before."

"Hello?" Rebekah moved a few steps down the hallway.

"See." Mouse shook his head. "No one is here."

Rebekah took a few more steps, then nodded. "Maybe you're right. It is an old house. It's probably just making noises. But I swear that I saw someone."

Another loud thump sounded right above them.

"What was that?" Mouse gasped as he looked up at the ceiling.

"I don't think she wants us to leave."

"Oh no, it came from the attic, didn't it?" Mouse winced. "That's not a good sign."

"That's where I saw her! In the attic window!"

"It could still just be an animal running around up there." Mouse stared at the ceiling. "How can we know for sure?"

"By having a look." Rebekah continued down the hallway. "But first we have to figure out how to get up there. There must be a door or a ladder somewhere."

"I'll look this way." Mouse walked the opposite way down the hall. He opened each door that he passed and peered inside.

Rebekah neared the last door at the end of the hallway. She grabbed the handle and pulled it open. Inside was a small closet that was just big enough for one person to stand in.

She looked down the hallway toward Mouse.

"Anything?"

"Not down here." Mouse pushed the last door on his side of the hallway closed.

"I don't understand. There has to be a way to get up there." Rebekah sighed and started to step out of the closet.

"Help!" A voice cried out from just above her head. "Please help! I'm up here!"

Rebekah jumped back, shocked by the girl's voice. "Mouse! Get down here quick!"

Mouse ran down the hallway to the closet where she stood. "What is it?"

"I heard her!" Rebekah jumped as high as she could and tried to touch the ceiling. "Hello? Are you there?"

"Look." Mouse pointed to a pole that leaned against the corner of the closet. "I bet that will go inside that hook." He looked up at the ceiling. "It must be the door to the attic. It blends in with the ceiling."

"Great job, Mouse!" Rebekah grabbed the pole.

"Wait!" Mouse's eyes widened. "We don't know what's really up there!"

SIX

"We have to try, Mouse! No matter who or what it is, she's asking for help!" Rebekah slipped the end of the pole through the hook and gave it a firm tug. The door wiggled, but it didn't open. "Mouse, help me with this. Please!"

"Absolutely." Mouse grabbed onto the pole as well.

Together they tugged and the door swung free of the ceiling.

"Watch out!" Rebekah gasped and pulled Mouse out of the way.

Wooden stairs unfolded and landed against the floor not far from where they had both been standing. A cloud of dust swirled through the air as they both peered up into the attic.

A shrill sound carried through the house.

"What's that?" Rebekah looked back down the hall. "Is that sirens?"

"Police sirens." Mouse cringed. "Rebekah, we have to get out of here. We can be arrested for trespassing!"

"Help!" the voice shouted again. "Please help!"

"See?" Rebekah looked at Mouse. "Someone is up there. We can't leave her here! We have to help!" She started up the rickety stairs.

"Be careful! I'm right behind you." Mouse climbed up behind her.

Rebekah poked her head through the opening of the attic. She peered through the dust and streams of sunlight that filtered through the small windows. All around were pieces of old furniture, cloths tossed over piles, and large boxes.

As she climbed off the stairs and into the attic, she saw someone move straight ahead of her, but she couldn't quite see her.

"Hello? We're here to help!"

Mouse climbed out behind her.

"Don't!" A girl jumped out from behind him.

Rebekah gasped.

The girl wore an old faded dress, similar to the ones that the staff of the village wore. Her dark hair was covered in dust, as was her face.

"No!" The girl let out a loud scream as the stairs folded back up and the door snapped shut. "What have you done?" Her scream became a shriek. "I've been trapped in here forever!"

"G-ghost!" Mouse stammered. "It's definitely a ghost!" He gulped, then crouched down to try to push the door open.

"Please don't be upset." Rebekah took a deep breath as she looked at the girl. "We're here to help you. It's been so long now, and I know that you want to be set free."

"Rebekah!" Mouse cried out as he looked up at her. "The door won't open!"

"What?" Rebekah crouched down and shoved the door hard. "Open!" She banged her fists against it.

"It's no use!" Mouse sank down to his knees, then looked into her eyes. "We're stuck up here—with a ghost!"

Rebekah looked back at the girl, who began to shriek again.

SEVEN

Rebekah's heart pounded as the girl shrieked.

"Please, calm down, we'll still help you! I know this was your house once, but it isn't anymore!"

The girl's shriek turned into loud laughter as she shook her head. "A ghost? You think I'm a ghost?" She rolled her eyes. "Ghosts aren't real!"

"You're not a ghost?" Mouse got back to his feet as he stared at her. "But you look like a ghost!"

"I wanted to fit in." She brushed some dust off the skirt of her dress. "I thought it would be fun to dress like they did in the past. Of course, I was the only one who dressed this way. A few of the kids from my school teased me about it."

"I saw you in the window. Were you waving to me?" Rebekah watched as the girl brushed some dust off of her face.

"Yes, I was waving to you—and to anyone else who might see me. I've been trying to find a way out of here. That's why I'm covered in dust. I thought when you saw me, you might help, but instead you've gotten us all trapped here!"

"I'm sorry, I didn't mean to." Rebekah sighed. "Wait, did you come up here alone?"

"Yes, I did." She walked over to a table and picked up a camera. "I thought I could get some great shots from up here. I'm doing a special project about the past, and I was hoping to find some antiques to get pictures of too. I thought this would be the perfect place. And I wanted to get away from those kids that wouldn't stop teasing me about my dress."

"I'm sorry they did that." Rebekah frowned. "I like your dress."

"Thanks." She smiled. "I made it myself."

"You're sure there's no one else up here?" Rebekah glanced around.

"Yes, why?"

"Because I saw someone else. When I first climbed in here. I saw someone move and it wasn't you."

"Maybe it's the real ghost?" Mouse gulped.

"I told you, ghosts aren't real. It's just me, Callie."

Rebekah shook her hand. "It's nice to meet you, Callie. I'm Rebekah and this is Mouse." She frowned. "Why did you say you were trapped here forever if you're not a ghost?"

"Well, since this morning." She shrugged. "I may have exaggerated a little, but it feels like forever. When I saw my bus drive away, I thought no one was ever going to find me. Then I heard voices and saw all of you down there. I thought maybe someone would see me."

"Don't worry." Mouse smiled at her. "We'll find a way out of here. Plus, when Mr. Cooper finds out we're missing, everyone will come looking for us."

"I thought the same about my principal." Callie crossed her arms. "But no one came."

"There!" Rebekah pointed straight ahead. "I just saw someone move again!"

EIGHT

"I saw something move too!" Mouse narrowed his eyes. "Someone else is up here with us!"

"Not a chance. I've been here for hours and I haven't seen anyone." Callie frowned. "Where did you see it?"

"There!" Rebekah pointed straight ahead to an area of the attic that the sunlight didn't reach.

"Let's see what it is." Callie took a step forward. "Let me guess, no one has their phones—or a flashlight?"

"No, our principal took them." Mouse sighed.

"I'm going to find out who would be up here sneaking around when someone needs help!" Rebekah stepped forward, determined to catch the culprit. As she stepped further into the darkness, she noticed a flicker of movement near the bottom of a cloth. Confused, she grabbed the cloth and whipped it away. "Got you!"

She gasped as wide eyes stared right back at her.

Callie began to shriek again—with laughter.

Mouse soon joined in.

Rebekah huffed and dropped the cloth, which had been covering a large mirror. "Okay, very funny! But let's not forget, we're all still stuck up here!" She turned around to face them. "Callie's right, we can't count on someone finding us. We have to find a way out."

"Maybe we can wave from the window again." Mouse walked over to the windows. "Oh no! Those really were police sirens we heard!"

"What's going on?" Rebekah peered out through the window. She saw a few police cars and all of the staff from the village, as well as Mr. Cooper, gathered together.

"Something big, that's for sure." Mouse winced.

"I bet they figured out that we're missing." She looked over at Callie. "Or maybe they figured out that you are missing!"

"It's about time!" She crossed her arms. "But that's not going to help if they don't know where to look for us!"

"Let's try to get their attention!" Rebekah pounded on the window.

Callie went to the other window and did the same.

"Help! Up here!" Mouse shouted as loud as he could.

Rebekah tried to pry the window open. "It's nailed shut!"

"They don't break either. I tried." Callie pointed to a heavy candlestick on the floor. "They must be made of extra thick glass."

"Hello!" Rebekah pounded and shouted.

Mr. Cooper looked up. He looked straight at her.

"Mr. Cooper!" She waved her hands wildly. "Up here!"

Mr. Cooper stared a moment longer, then looked away.

"I know he saw me!" Rebekah frowned.

"Look how sunny it is, Rebekah. I couldn't see Callie when the sun was shining on the window, remember?" Mouse frowned. "He probably can't see us. None of them can."

"How are we ever going to get out of here?" Callie moaned.

"I have an idea." Rebekah looked at Callie. "But I'm going to need your help."

NINE

"Of course I'll help. But I'm not sure how." Callie looked out through the window. "I've been trying to get out of here all day, and you're the only one who saw me."

"But I did see you!" Rebekah smiled. "Which means it's not impossible. We just need to find a way to get their attention, and I think your camera might be the key. Can I see it?"

"What are you going to do with it?" Callie frowned as she handed it over. "It's very important to me."

"Don't worry, I won't break it." Rebekah looked it over. "It has a flash, doesn't it?"

"Yes."

"Oh, good idea, Rebekah!" Mouse nodded. "A flash might get someone's attention!"

"Yes, but we need it to go off more than once or they will just think it's the sunlight." She handed the camera back to Callie. "Can you make it do that?"

"There's a setting to take lots of pictures in a row." Callie pressed a few buttons on the camera. "Hopefully this will work!" She walked over to the window.

"Wait for me to say go. I want to make sure there are people looking this way when we start."

Rebekah peered down at the crowd below. Mr. Cooper waved his arms in the air and appeared to be shouting at one of the police officers. She could only imagine what he might be saying—probably something about herself and Mouse being nothing but trouble.

She shook her head. All that mattered was getting out of the attic.

She banged on the window a few times. Mr. Cooper suddenly turned his head toward the house. A few other people in the crowd looked toward the attic at the same time.

"Now!" Rebekah gasped. "Do it now, Callie!"

The attic filled with bright light as the flash began to go off over and over again. Callie kept the camera pointed toward the window, while Mouse and Rebekah slammed their hands against the other window and shouted.

Mr. Cooper ran toward the house, followed by a few police officers and staff members.

"Yes!" Mouse grinned as he jumped up and down. "They saw us! We did it!"

"Finally!" Callie sighed as she lowered her camera. "Now we just have to make sure they don't get stuck up here too!"

"You're right." Mouse ran over to the attic door. He shouted as loud as he could. "We're up here! We're not ghosts!"

Rebekah followed after them. She was glad to have been rescued, but she also knew that they were going to be in big trouble. She'd seen how angry Mr. Cooper was when he talked to the police officer. She could only guess that he was going to be just as angry as soon as they were out of the attic.

"They're in the attic!" Mr. Cooper's voice bellowed from the hallway. "Hurry! Someone get this open right now!"

"Watch out!" Mouse shooed Rebekah and Callie away from

the attic door as it swung open. The steps unfolded with a clatter. A flashlight beam pointed up into the attic.

"Rebekah? Mouse?" Mr. Cooper called out.

"Yes, we're here! And Callie is too!" Rebekah shouted down to him. "The door gets stuck! Don't let it close!"

TEN

"Can you climb down?" Mr. Cooper looked up the stairs at them.

"Sure, we can." Rebekah laughed nervously. She looked at Mouse.

"We're going to have to go down sometime." Mouse shrugged.

"I'll go." Callie started down the steps.

Mouse climbed down after her.

Rebekah followed behind him.

"Callie!" A woman rushed forward and pulled the girl into a tight hug. "We were all so worried about you! I'm so sorry, we must have lost count when we loaded the bus. Are you okay?"

"I'm fine, Mrs. Blue." She smiled. "But I am a little hungry."

"Let's get you something to eat—some ice cream—does that sound good?" Mrs. Blue escorted her down the hallway.

"Ice cream sounds good." Mouse smiled.

"Wait a minute." Mr. Cooper clapped his hand on Mouse's shoulder. "You two aren't going anywhere."

Rebekah looked at Mouse.

Mouse winced.

"Why don't you tell me exactly what happened here?" Mr. Cooper crossed his arms. "Didn't you know that this house was off limits?"

Rebekah took a deep breath. "Yes, Mr. Cooper, we did know that, but I saw Callie in the window. I thought she might need our help. Mouse only came with me because I begged him. It wasn't his fault."

"If you saw her in the window, why didn't you tell me?" Mr. Cooper frowned. "When the police arrived to look for Callie, I realized the two of you were missing too. Do you have any idea how scary that was?"

"I'm sorry, Mr. Cooper." Rebekah frowned. "I just wanted to help Callie."

"And I'm glad you did. You two were both very brave and you did help rescue her. But you didn't answer my question. Why didn't you tell me what you saw, Rebekah?"

"I didn't think you'd believe me." Rebekah shrugged.

"That's a problem, isn't it?" He looked between the two of them. "I'm your principal—do you know what that means?"

"Detention?" Mouse squeaked.

"No, Mouse." Mr. Cooper shook his head. "It means that I'm here to help you and to keep you safe. If you tell me something is wrong, I will help."

Rebekah looked at Mouse.

Mouse smiled. "So, no detention?"

"No detention, Mouse." Mr. Cooper sighed. "But next time, you both need to come to me. It wasn't safe for you to come into this house alone. You could have been hurt."

"Or left behind like Callie." Mouse frowned.

"No." Mr. Cooper shook his head. "No, I would never forget about you two. Now go on, get some ice cream with the other kids. This field trip is over."

"Yes! Ice cream!" Mouse took off down the hall.

"No running, Mouse!" Mr. Cooper called out.

Rebekah followed after Mouse. She reached the top of the porch steps, then paused. She looked back at Mr. Cooper.

He held something in his hand—something round and shiny with a chain that hung from it. He stared down at it for a long moment, then tucked it into his pocket. He looked up and spotted her watching.

Rebekah gulped, then bolted down the stairs.

Mr. Cooper had said that they weren't in trouble, but she wasn't so sure. What was it that he'd held in his hand?

As she and Mouse walked away from the old house, a cheer went up through the crowd outside.

Callie had shared the story about her rescue.

A few of the police officers shook their hands.

"Your principal was so worried about you." One of the officers smiled at Rebekah. "I'm glad you're all okay."

Rebekah smiled at the officer and let herself feel the sense of pride that she often felt after solving a mystery. She pulled her notebook out of her backpack.

Yes, the mystery of the girl in the window had been solved, but she now had some new notes to make about Principal Cooper.

BOOK 4: THE MYSTERIOUS BOOK

ONE

Rebekah glanced at her watch. She only had a few more minutes to find what she needed. She and her friend Mouse had stayed after school to use the library, but soon it would be closing.

"I know it's here somewhere." Rebekah looked down at the slip of paper in her hand, then back up at the row of books in front of her. "*Great Detectives Throughout History*. Do you see it, Mouse?"

"No, sorry." Mouse peered at a set of books on the shelf. "But these look pretty interesting. *Great Dinosaurs Throughout Time*."

"Fine, fine, read about dinosaurs if you want, but I want a book about detectives. I need to step up my skills a bit. I feel like I'm getting rusty."

"You? Rusty?" Mouse laughed.

"Shh!" the librarian called out from the big circular desk she sat behind.

"Sorry." Mouse frowned, then lowered his voice. "Rebekah, you are the best detective I know."

"What about my cousin, RJ?" Rebekah raised an eyebrow.

"Well, RJ is pretty good too, but he's no Rebekah, girl detective." Mouse grinned.

"A great detective knows that she can only get greater! That's why I need this book—so that I can see if I'm missing any skills. I want to make sure that there is no mystery I can't solve." She ran her fingertips along the books and sighed. "But apparently I'm not even a good enough detective to find the book I'm looking for."

"Maybe it's not even here." Mouse shrugged. "You know the books can get misfiled sometimes."

"That's true. I could ask Mrs. Nix if she knows where it is." Rebekah looked over at the librarian, who had her nose tucked into a very thick book. "But she seems a bit busy. I think I'll just keep looking." She smiled as she took a deep breath. "I love the way the library smells."

"That's a little strange." Mouse unzipped the pouch he wore around his waist and put a bit of cracker inside.

"Not as strange as feeding your pouch crackers." Rebekah grinned.

"Magellan gets noisy when he gets hungry. He's not exactly the best at being quiet in libraries." He gave the mouse a light petting, then zipped the pouch back up.

Rebekah barely heard him as her eyes settled on a book. Golden swirls decorated its spine. Once she saw it, she felt as if she couldn't look away. Her heart skipped a beat as she traced her fingertip across the book's spine. "What is this?"

"Did you find it?" Mouse looked over her shoulder at the book.

"No, but I found something." She pulled the book off the shelf. "Mouse, look at this!" She ran her fingertips across colored stones that decorated the cover of the book. Each one was a different color, and all were slightly different in size. "Have you ever seen anything like this?"

"Only in movies!" His eyes widened as he looked at the stones. "Do you think they're real gems?"

TWO

"No, I doubt they're real. I don't think anyone would put a book with real gemstones on it in a library." Rebekah squinted at the gold lettering on the brown cover of the book. "I think these are letters, but not any that I can read. Can you?"

"Maybe that's an 'a'?" Mouse shook his head. "I'm not sure. It's so curly."

"I think it might be a different language." Rebekah flipped the book open. The first page had a small card inside. On the card, two letters were written. "KC." She looked up at Mouse. "I wonder what that means?"

"Maybe it's just a bookmark." Mouse shrugged.

"It's definitely a different language." Rebekah flipped through a few more of the pages. "I've never seen a language like this, though. I can't make anything of it." She sighed. "I wish I could understand it. I bet it's a really interesting book."

"The library is closing, kids!" Mrs. Nix called out from her desk. "If you have anything to check out, please bring it to me now."

"Oh no, I never found my book!" Rebekah frowned, then she looked down at the book in her hands. "But maybe I found a better one. What better way to improve my detective skills than to figure out what this language is and where it comes from?"

"Sounds like a good idea to me." Mouse pointed to a group of symbols on one of the pages. "Maybe these symbols will give us a clue as to where the book was written."

"It could be a good start." Rebekah nodded. She walked up to the check-out desk and set the book down on it. "I'd like to check out this book please, Mrs. Nix."

"Oh, isn't this interesting?" Mrs. Nix tilted her head to the side. "It's pretty odd-looking, isn't it?"

"A bit." Rebekah nodded. "I'm quite curious about it."

Mrs. Nix flipped the book open and stared down at the inside of the cover. "Oh dear."

"What's wrong?" Rebekah frowned.

"I'm sorry, Rebekah, but I can't check this book out to you." She closed the book again.

"Why not?" Rebekah held out her library card. "I have my card with me."

"That's good, but I still can't check it out. This isn't a library book." She pointed to the empty inside cover. "See? It doesn't have a barcode for me to scan. Someone must have left this behind."

"But it was on a shelf."

"Maybe someone put it there by mistake." Mrs. Nix shook her head. "There's nothing I can do."

"Can I still take it with me?" Rebekah picked the book up. "I'm sure someone is missing it. I'm a detective, I can figure out who it belongs to."

"I suppose that's a good idea then." Mrs. Nix smiled. "I'm sure you will find the owner in no time." She looked up at the clock on the wall. "Okay, closing time, kids. Good luck with your mystery!"

THREE

Rebekah tucked the book into her backpack right next to her detective's notebook. Her fingers itched to pull it out and start making notes on the latest mystery she'd uncovered.

"We'd better go, Rebekah." Mouse nudged her with his elbow. "We don't want to get trapped at school, do we?"

"No, I guess not. Want to come over and look at the book some more?" She led the way out the door.

"Sure. I bet we can find out more about what language the book is written in with a little internet search." Mouse waved to a few kids as they headed down the sidewalk toward Rebekah's house. "Maybe if we can figure that out, we'll get an idea of where this book came from and who lost it."

Rebekah stepped up onto the front porch of her house and opened the door. "What kind of person has a book like that?"

"What kind of person loses a book like that?" Mouse shook his head. "If I had a book like that, I would never leave it behind!"

Rebekah sat down on the sofa and pulled the book out of her backpack. She set it on the cushion between her and Mouse, then pulled out her detective's notebook.

"Okay, we have to make sure we get all the facts straight." She began writing down notes. "We found the book in the library on the shelf. It's not a library book. We need to find out where the book came from and who lost it." She looked up at Mouse. "Does that about cover it?"

"I think so." Mouse flipped the book open and snapped a picture of the text inside. "If I do an internet search on this picture, I might be able to find out what language this is."

"That would be great." Rebekah closed the book. "I want to add some drawings and measurements of the stones on the front." She began to sketch out the shape of the stones in her notebook.

"Got it. I think." Mouse frowned as he looked at his phone. "According to this, the book is written in an ancient language that isn't even spoken anymore."

"Really?" Rebekah peered at the book. "Then it must be very old."

"The letters look about the same." Mouse held out his phone.

"Yes, you're right." Rebekah looked through the pictures. "Great job, Mouse! You've found our first clue!"

"Maybe, but it's the oldest clue ever!" Mouse laughed. "I'd better get home. Good luck with the mystery, Rebekah."

"Thanks!" She pulled the book into her lap and looked at the card on the inside cover again. "KC. Is this your book, KC?"

FOUR

Rebekah flipped through the pages of the book. She noticed how thin and old the paper seemed to be. She stared hard at the strange letters and wished she could read the words.

"What secrets do you hold, book? How did you end up in the library?"

She closed the book and set it on her bedside table. She turned out her light and closed her eyes. It was late and she wanted to sleep, but she couldn't. Her thoughts ran wild with possibilities.

How had the book ended up at her school? It looked so magical. Was it some kind of magic book? Had a wizard from the past somehow sent the book through time just for her to find?

As she drifted off to sleep, she tried to imagine the type of wizard that might do this.

"Rebekah!"

She jerked at the sound of someone calling out her name.

She opened her eyes and saw her dark bedroom all around her.

The sun hadn't come up yet. So why was she awake?

"Rebekah!" The voice came from a corner of her room.

"Who's there?" Her heart pounded as she sat up.

"You found my book." A figure stepped forward.

Rebekah squinted, but she couldn't see through the darkness. "Who are you?"

"That doesn't matter. All that matters is who you are!"

"What?" She rubbed her eyes. "I'm just Rebekah."

"Oh? Do I have the wrong house? The wrong time? The wrong girl? I thought I sent my book to the greatest girl detective of her time!"

"Oh—uh—well." Rebekah smiled. "I mean, I am a pretty good detective."

"No, I didn't send my book to a pretty *good* detective. I must have gotten my signals crossed. I'll just take it back now."

"No!" Rebekah reached for the book. Certain she had left it on her bedside table, she found nothing but her alarm clock and a few tiny figurines. "Where is it?"

"Like I said, it's supposed to go to the greatest girl detective. Only she will be able to find its true owner!"

"That's me!" Rebekah jumped up on her bed and stared at the figure, still hidden in the shadows. "I'll find who it belongs to! I promise!"

"Are you sure?"

"Absolutely! You can count on me!"

"Alright then. Hurry up, will you?" The figure suddenly disappeared.

Rebekah blinked. She stared up at her ceiling. A yawn pushed past her lips.

Had it just been a dream? She gasped and looked over at her bedside table. The book was right where she'd left it.

As sunlight peeked through her bedroom window, she jumped out of bed.

She *was* the greatest girl detective and she had a job to do!

FIVE

"Mouse, you will not believe the dream I had!" Rebekah grinned as she ran up to him at the corner of their street.

"I might if you tell me." He laughed. "It must have been very good."

"It was." She filled him in about the dream as they walked to school.

"I would have been a little scared having a strange wizard in my room." Mouse raised an eyebrow. "You weren't?"

"No, I only got scared when he said he was going to take the book away. I was so glad to see it when I woke up." She rubbed her arms. "It gave me goosebumps. I really think it's important that we return the book to its owner. Maybe it was just a dream. Maybe there is no magical wizard, but I am still a detective, and it is still my job to make sure the book gets back to the right place."

"You're right about that." He tilted his head side to side. "But maybe it wasn't a dream."

"Either way, I have a job to do." She walked into the school with Mouse right behind her. "I was thinking the letters that we found inside the book might be initials. What do you think?"

"Maybe. It's hard to say, but it's definitely possible. It might be a good place to start." He scratched his head. "I don't think we're going to be able to translate any of the text, so that might not lead us anywhere."

"I think I'll go back to the library and look around. If the book was lost there, maybe whoever lost it left something else behind too."

"Good luck. I have to help Mr. Bromley set up the science experiment today." Mouse waved to her as he walked off down the hall. "Let me know what you find!"

"I will!"

Rebekah walked toward the library. As the hallway became more crowded with kids, she tried to focus on the task at hand.

Sure, she was a great detective, but she had a feeling this would be a hard case to crack.

She was almost to the library when someone pushed past her.

She stepped back as Mr. Cooper whirled around to face her.

"Rebekah! Please be more careful. Watch where you're going!"

Rebekah stared at him, wide-eyed. He had been the one to bump into her. Why did he think it was her fault?

He stared at her a moment longer, then hurried down the hall.

Rebekah frowned as she watched him stride away. Mr. Cooper was one of those mysteries that she had not been able to solve.

As a principal, he was quite strange. Sometimes he seemed fun, playing along or being silly. Other times he seemed stern. She'd started taking notes about him in her detective's notebook during the first week of school, but she still hadn't figured him out.

From the way he stormed down the hall, she could tell that he was upset about something.

"Alright, Mr. Cooper, let's see what you're up to." Rebekah followed after him.

SIX

Mr. Cooper stepped into the library and headed straight for the shelves in the back.

Rebekah stepped into the library as well. She ducked between two shelves and watched as Mr. Cooper began walking up and down the next aisle.

Moments later the bell rang.

Mr. Cooper looked up at the sound.

Rebekah knelt down.

Had he seen her? She sighed as she realized that she couldn't be late to class.

She took one last look at Mr. Cooper, who had turned back to the shelves.

"Rebekah!" Mrs. Nix called out from her desk. "You need to get to class or you'll be late!"

Rebekah grimaced. There was no doubt in her mind that Mr. Cooper had heard Mrs. Nix say her name. Already he thought she had bumped into him, and now he very likely suspected that she intended to skip class.

"On my way, Mrs. Nix, thanks!" Rebekah waved to her as she hurried out the door.

She didn't dare look back to see if Mr. Cooper had spotted her.

When she arrived to class, she found Mouse waiting for her.

"What happened?" He frowned. "You are cutting it really close."

"I know." She settled at her desk, then told him about her encounter with Mr. Cooper. "He seemed really upset about something."

"Hmm. Maybe it has something to do with the men in suits I saw walking around school this morning." He raised his eyebrows. "Fancy suits always mean something bad."

"What do you mean?"

"Well, the only people who wear suits like that are bosses, and the only time bosses seem to show up is when someone is in trouble."

"You think Mr. Cooper could be in trouble?" Rebekah laughed. "He's the principal. What could he be in trouble for?"

"I don't know, but with that many suits around, I'd guess it's something pretty bad." Mouse frowned. "Maybe he's going to be fired."

"What could he have done to make that happen?" Rebekah shook her head.

"You two in the back, quiet down please!"

Rebekah nodded to the teacher, then sank down in her seat.

Sure, she suspected that Mr. Cooper was hiding something, but that didn't mean she wanted him to be fired. So far, he hadn't really been a bad principal, just a strange one. What if he got replaced by someone far worse?

She dug out her detective's notebook and added notes to two cases.

First, she added a note about Mr. Cooper looking through the shelves in the library. Was he looking for the book?

Then she flipped to Mr. Cooper's case and added a note about him possibly being fired.

By the end of class, she was determined to find out what kind of trouble Mr. Cooper might be in as well as who the book belonged to.

When the bell rang, she jumped out of her seat.

"Rebekah, slow down!" Mouse followed her into the hall. "What are you doing?"

"I'm going on a principal hunt!"

SEVEN

Rebekah looked at the clock on the wall. "I only have a few minutes between classes to get a little more information."

"Don't be late." Mouse shook his head. "I'm sure that Mr. Cooper wouldn't be too happy about that."

"I won't be, I promise." She waved to him as he walked the other way down the hall.

While the other kids began to step into their classrooms, Rebekah searched the halls for Mr. Cooper.

She finally found him near the front of the school. She watched as he popped open a locker and peered inside. He slammed it shut, then opened the next one.

Rebekah glanced at the clock. She only had about a minute to get across the school to her class. But how could she walk away without knowing what Mr. Cooper was up to? If he really was in some kind of trouble, maybe she could help.

"Mr. Cooper?"

He jumped, then spun around to face her. "Rebekah, you should be in class."

"I'm on my way! Just got a little turned around." She looked into his eyes. "Mr. Cooper, what are you doing?"

"I'm conducting a locker search." He cleared his throat. "It's something principals do once in a while."

"But why are you doing it?" Rebekah frowned. "Is something wrong?"

"Rebekah, it really isn't any of your business. Now you'd better hurry if you're going to get to class on time." He pulled open another locker.

"Maybe if you tell me what's going on, I can help you." Rebekah smiled. "I am a detective, you know."

"So I've heard." He looked straight at her.

Rebekah's heart pounded. "A good one."

"I'm sure you are, Rebekah. I've lost something and I will find it. No mystery for you to solve here, I'm afraid." He frowned as the bell rang. "Now you're late."

"I'm going!" Rebekah ran down the hall.

"Rebekah!" Mr. Cooper shouted. "No running!"

She slowed down, until she turned the corner. Then she began to run again. She ducked into her classroom, out of breath and sweaty.

"Rebekah, it's about time you showed up." Her art teacher sighed. "I'll let you slide this time, but no more being late. Understood?"

"Yes, of course. I'm so sorry." Rebekah settled at her desk and picked up her sketch pad.

As she began to sketch what she imagined the wizard from her dream to look like, she thought about what Mr. Cooper had said about losing something that he had to find.

When the bell rang for lunch, Rebekah spotted Mouse at their table. She sat down across from him and reached into her backpack.

"Mouse, I think I might know who this book belongs to."

"You do?" Mouse's eyes widened. "That was fast."

EIGHT

"I found Mr. Cooper in the hall doing a locker search. He said that he lost something and that he has to find it. He was also in the library this morning looking for something. I think maybe the book belongs to him." She set the book on the table between them and opened it up. She pointed to the card with the letters KC on it. "Maybe the C stands for Cooper?"

"It could be." Mouse nodded, then narrowed his eyes. "But why would Mr. Cooper have a book like this?"

"Remember when we were trapped in the attic on our last field trip?" Rebekah flipped her detective's notebook open to the section on Mr. Cooper. "I saw him holding something strange." She pointed to the sketch she'd drawn of the medallion. "It looked old and expensive. This book is very old too. Maybe he's some kind of wizard."

"Mr. Cooper?" Mouse laughed. "No way, he's just the principal."

"Think about it. He's not like any other principal we've ever had. He's pretty weird. What if he is a wizard and this is his book?"

"Well, I'm not saying you're wrong. You're usually right,

after all. But just think about this. If you were some great and powerful wizard and you had a magical book, why would you ever be a principal?" Mouse shook his head. "It just doesn't add up."

"You're right." She sighed and slumped back in her chair. A second later her eyes widened. "Unless!" She held one finger up in the air.

"Unless what?" Mouse stared at her.

"Unless he's planning to use that magical book to put a spell on a school full of children!" She smacked her hand against the table. "I bet that's it! That's why he's so strange. He's not here to be our principal at all, Mouse! He's here because he is up to something terrible, and we are the only ones who can stop him!"

"Wait a minute!" Mouse held up his hands. "Now you know I'm not a fan of Mr. Cooper's. He is always trying to find out about Magellan. But that doesn't make him some kind of evil wizard."

"You're right." Rebekah frowned. "I have a hunch, but I don't have any evidence to back it up. If I'm going to prove that he's a wizard who's up to no good, then we're going to need more evidence."

"How are we going to get that?" Mouse slipped a few pieces of his cheese into Magellan's pouch.

"First things first. We need to find out what Mr. Cooper's first name is." She stood up from her chair. "If it starts with a K then we might be on to something."

"You know finding out an adult's first name isn't easy." Mouse stood up as well. "They always want to be called Mr. So-and-so. How are we going to do it?"

"Follow me!" Rebekah grinned. "Detectives always know where to look!"

NINE

"What does that mean exactly, Rebekah?"

She grabbed his hand and pulled him down the hallway. "We have to hurry, or we might miss our chance!"

"Our chance to what?" Mouse stumbled over his feet as he tried to keep up.

"Great, it looks like Ms. Wentworth is at lunch." Rebekah poked her head into the office at the front of the school. She looked back over her shoulder at Mouse. "I'm sure we can find some paperwork that has his first name on it. We just have to look through some of the papers on Ms. Wentworth's desk."

"Alright, I'll keep watch for her." Mouse peered down the hallway. "Uh-oh." He took a step back. "The men in fancy suits are headed this way."

"Hurry, get behind the door!" Rebekah grabbed Mouse's arm and pulled him behind the door of the office. She put her finger to her lips.

Mouse nodded, then stood perfectly still.

Three men in suits walked past the office door to the door that led to Principal Cooper's office. The tallest of the group knocked firmly on the door.

Rebekah peered through the crack between the wall and the door and watched as Mr. Cooper's door swung open.

"Please, if you could just be a little more patient, I'm sure that I will find it."

"We've been patient, Kevin!" The tall man frowned.

"We came a long way for this." A shorter man beside him sighed.

"How could you lose something so valuable?" The roundest man of the three shook his head. "We thought you were trustworthy, but clearly you are not. We're going to have to report this."

"Wait, please." Mr. Cooper gestured for them to enter his office. "Let's talk about this a bit more. In private." As the three men filed into his office, Mr. Cooper looked both ways down the hall. Then he pulled his office door shut.

"Hey, Rebekah," Mouse whispered.

"What?" Rebekah whispered back.

"I think Mr. Cooper's first name is Kevin."

"Mouse, you are a fantastic detective." Rebekah rolled her eyes as she laughed. "Kevin Cooper. KC. It really is his book." She led Mouse out into the hallway. "And it sounds like it's very important—and very valuable."

"And it sounds like Mr. Cooper is in big trouble." Mouse frowned. "That's never fun, even for adults."

"What are we going to do?" Rebekah unzipped her backpack and looked inside. "What if it is magical and he plans to use it on everyone in our school?"

"If it is magical, it's probably not the only magical thing he has. Besides, we don't know if it is. All we know is that he lost it, we found it, and it belongs to him."

"You're right." She frowned. "But we can't just give it back to him. If he finds out we're the ones who found it, he might think we know his secret."

"What are we going to do?" Mouse sighed.

"I have a plan." Rebekah smiled.

TEN

"Why?" Mouse moaned as he walked beside Rebekah after their last class of the day. "Why do your plans always involve Magellan?"

"I can't help it. He's a big part of my team." She grinned.

"But if Mr. Cooper sees me with him, he's going to use that spell book to turn me into a mouse too!"

"Don't worry, Mouse, I won't let that happen." She looked into his eyes. "I promise."

"And how are you going to stop it from happening?"

"All you have to do is let Magellan run free in the office for just a minute. That will send Ms. Wentworth into a frenzy, and with all the kids leaving school for the day, there will be enough of a crowd for her to lose track of him. I'm sure Mr. Cooper will want to see what all the commotion is about. That will give me a chance to get inside his office and put the book in there." She shook her head. "We'll just have to hope it's not a spell book."

"Alright, but you'll have to be quick. If Mr. Cooper catches you, he's not going to believe any of your excuses."

"You're probably right." She nodded.

"Don't worry, we can handle this!" Mouse pulled Magellan out of his pouch. "Right, buddy?"

Magellan's nose twitched.

"Thanks, Magellan." Rebekah leaned against the wall just beside Mr. Cooper's office. She looked over at the door that led to the main office and nodded to Mouse.

Mouse took a deep breath, then stepped inside.

Seconds later, Rebekah heard the scream, followed by a crash. Several people in the main office bolted out of it into the hallway.

"What's going on out here?" Mr. Cooper stepped out of his office and hurried over to the main office. "Ms. Wentworth, are you okay?"

"Mouse!" She shrieked as she pointed into the office.

"Great, what did he do now?" Mr. Cooper sighed.

"No, not that Mouse." Ms. Wentworth waved her hands through the air. "A real mouse!"

Rebekah slipped into Mr. Cooper's office. Her heart raced because she knew that she didn't have much time.

She pulled the book out of her backpack and set it on top of Mr. Cooper's desk. As she did, she noticed a piece of paper next to his keyboard. It had a note scribbled across it.

"Ancient tomb of peace?" She looked from the note to the book, then back to the note. "To be viewed by the Committee." She shook her head. "I doubt a spell book would be called ancient tomb of peace."

She took a step back from the desk and noticed all of the statues that lined the shelves. Some of them were large and golden, while others were small and appeared to be made of clay. They were all different shapes and colors.

"I don't have time to sketch all this!" She frowned.

She spun around slowly and took in the sight of a wall of

books, all just as strange and beautiful as the one she had just placed on Mr. Cooper's desk.

"Mr. Cooper, what kind of principal are you?" Her gaze settled on a large sphere on one of the shelves. Dark blue and sparkly, it caught and reflected light in a dazzling way.

Before she had a chance to wonder what it was, she heard footsteps headed toward the door.

She ran out of the office just as Mr. Cooper turned toward it.

"I don't have time for this! I have to find my book!"

"Did he see you?" Mouse zipped Magellan's pouch shut as he ran up to Rebekah.

"I don't think so."

"Yes!" Mr. Cooper's voice boomed from inside his office. "I found it!"

Rebekah glanced at Mouse, who smiled back at her.

Yes, they'd solved one mystery, but after seeing what was inside Mr. Cooper's office, Rebekah knew there was a lot more to discover about her principal.

BOOK 5: SOCCER SPIES

ONE

Rebekah tightened the laces on her soccer shoes, then looked up at her teammates all around her. Now that it was soccer season, she was so excited to get out on the field with all of her friends.

She looked out over the green soccer field and smiled. Mr. Cooper, the principal of her school, had made sure the sports fields were in top condition at their new school.

As a detective, Rebekah had a lot of questions about him and his strange behavior, but she was grateful that he had done so much work on the sports fields. She jumped to her feet and ran out on the field.

"Remember, girls, this is just a practice game, but we want to really tighten up our skills after being off all summer. So, give it your all!" Coach Nina waved to them as they took their positions on the field.

Rebekah dug her cleats into the grass, eager to get started.

Although she spent most of her time doing detective work, she did enjoy getting onto the soccer field where all her focus was on making a goal.

Coach Nina blew the whistle and Rebekah launched into action. She charged across the field and kept her eyes open for the ball. Even though soccer wasn't exactly solving a mystery, she could still find clues about where the ball would be based on who had it and where they kicked it.

As the ball sailed in her direction, excitement bolted through her.

This would be her chance to show the team that she'd practiced and kept her skills up over the summer, even while she was at summer camp.

She ran toward the ball, her focus on its spin and exactly where she wanted to kick it. As she struck it with her foot, she felt the impact and knew that she'd hit it in the right direction.

She kicked the ball as she ran straight toward the goal. The goalie crouched down, ready to block it.

Rebekah knew she could get it past her. She just had to kick the ball at the right angle. She drew her foot back, prepared to strike, and looked up straight ahead at exactly where she wanted the ball to go.

As she did, she caught sight of something very strange hovering in the air. As her mind tried to make sense of what it was, she didn't notice what the rest of her body was doing. Her foot connected with the ball as her body lunged forward.

She didn't realize that she'd lost her balance until it was too late to catch it. As her knee struck the ground, she heard the groans of her teammates. But her eyes were glued to the circular thing in the sky.

When pain bolted through her knee, she gasped and realized that time hadn't stopped. She'd kicked the ball way off to the side of the goal. One of her teammates was still running after it but it was now out of bounds.

TWO

Rebekah ignored the pain in her knee as she got to her feet. She looked back up at the sky in search of the strange object that she'd seen.

All she saw was bright blue sky in every direction.

"Did you see that?"

"See you kick the ball in the wrong direction?" Fran rolled her eyes as she ran up to her. "Yes, I saw it. What happened? Are you hurt?"

Rebekah glanced at her knee, then shook her head. "No, I'm okay. I saw something really strange in the sky. Didn't any of you see it?"

"Rebekah, we're in the middle of a game!" Fran sighed. "Pay attention, you already missed one goal!"

Rebekah gulped as she realized the game was still in motion all around her.

Coach Nina waved to her from the edge of the field. "Get moving, Rebekah! No standing still!"

Embarrassed, but also very curious, Rebekah couldn't help but look at the sky again. She knew that she'd seen something, and that something wasn't anything that should have been in the sky. Even if none of her friends had seen it, she was sure that it had been there.

"Rebekah!" Chelsea bumped into her from behind. "If you're not going to play, get off the field!"

Rebekah shook her head, then took off after the ball.

She certainly hadn't shown off her soccer skills. In fact, she wasn't sure if Coach Nina would keep her on the team now. As disappointing as that was, she still wanted to find out more about what she had seen.

When the game ended, Rebekah ran right over to her backpack on the sidelines.

"Rebekah, what happened out there?" Coach Nina walked up to her.

"I'm sorry, Coach. I guess I got distracted." Rebekah glanced up at the sky again.

"Listen, I know it's our first real practice, but you need to show me that you're committed to playing. There are other girls that may want to take your spot if you're not."

"I am, Coach Nina. I promise." Rebekah frowned. "I won't let it happen again."

"Okay. Don't worry about today. We're all a little rusty." The coach gave her a light pat on the shoulder.

Rebekah sighed as she pulled her detective's notebook out of her backpack. She was going to have to make things right with her team, but at the moment, she had a mystery to focus on.

She flipped to a fresh page and began to jot down notes about what she'd seen in the sky. Then she started to sketch what she remembered. She wrote down each color she saw next to the spot on the circle where she'd seen it. As she stared at the object on her page, she still didn't have any idea what it might be.

"Hey, Rebekah." A bright pink slushie appeared in front of her face. "I thought you might need this."

THREE

"Thanks, Mouse." Rebekah sighed as she took the slushie from him. "I guess you heard?"

"I ran into Chelsea at the store and she told me that practice didn't go too well for you. Are you okay?" He sat down on the bench beside her. "I know you were excited about playing today."

"I'm alright. I just got distracted." She smiled as she took a sip of her slushie. "We have a new mystery to solve."

"The mystery of the missing soccer goal?" Mouse laughed.

"Very funny!" Rebekah rolled her eyes. "Some best friend you are."

"Hey, I brought you your favorite slushie, didn't I?" He grinned.

"True, you really are a great best friend." She took another sip, then handed him her notebook. He was the only one that ever got to see her notes. "Take a look at this and tell me what you think it might be.

"A UFO? You saw a UFO?" Mouse jumped up from the bench. "Yes! I knew they were real!"

"Huh? A UFO?"

"Yeah, you know—unidentified flying object! Like from outer space!"

Rebekah peered at the picture. "No, I don't think so. It was too small to be a UFO."

"Maybe it's a tiny UFO." Mouse turned the notebook to the side to look at the sketch from a different angle. "We don't know how big aliens might be. They could be as tiny as ants."

"I don't know." Rebekah frowned. "It was really strange. No one else saw it! Then it just seemed to vanish."

"What else could it be then?" Mouse frowned.

"Maybe some kind of flying toy? Like a remote-controlled helicopter?" She shook her head. "But it didn't look like a helicopter."

"Hmm." Mouse looked at the sketch again. "I guess it could be something like that. But how did it disappear so fast?"

Rebekah looked up at the soccer field again. "Maybe it didn't disappear. Maybe I just didn't see it fly behind those trees. I was too busy checking on my knee." She brushed off a bit of dirt and frowned. "Looks like it's going to bruise a bit."

"Put your slushie on it." Mouse smiled. "That should help."

"Good idea." Rebekah pressed the cold cup against her knee. "Yes, that's much better!" She sighed. "So, it could be some kind of remote-control plane, but why would it be flying around our soccer field?"

"Oh, Rebekah!" Mouse gasped. "Maybe what you saw was some kind of spy tool!"

"You think someone was spying on our soccer game?" She laughed. "Who would want to do that?" Suddenly her eyes narrowed. "The Leprechauns!"

"What?" Mouse stared at her. "You think leprechauns are spying on you? As in little guys in green hats with pots of gold?"

"More like girls in green and gold uniforms!" Rebekah stood up. "I know exactly who was spying on me today, and they're the reason I missed my goal and hurt my knee!"

"The leprechauns?" Mouse squeaked.

FOUR

"Yes, the Leprechauns!" Rebekah sighed. "Are you listening? The soccer team from the next town is called the Lofton Leprechauns! Our first real game is against them next week!"

"I'm not saying it's not possible, Rebekah, but have you really thought about the UFO idea? I mean, if I was a tiny alien, I might want to check out what all of those giants in uniforms were doing on a soccer field. Right?"

"Right, Mouse." Rebekah frowned. "I can't be certain that it's the Leprechauns, but I do think there's a better chance that it could be them. If they want to beat us, then finding out some of our moves and how we practice would really help them do that."

"But it would also be cheating." Mouse narrowed his eyes. "It wouldn't be fair."

"No, it wouldn't. But people don't always do the right thing." Rebekah slurped the last of her slushie. "Let's go back to my house. Maybe we can find out a little more about what I saw."

"I'll keep an eye on the sky." Mouse started walking toward

the road. With his eyes glued to the sky, he tripped on the curb at the edge of the field.

Rebekah caught him before he fell. "Mouse, maybe keep your eyes off the sky." Rebekah laughed. "I don't think it's going to come back. Whoever is behind it—or in it—might know that I spotted it."

"That's a good point. Maybe you scared them off. But I hope not. I'd love to meet a real alien."

"What would you say to one if you did?" Rebekah walked quickly down the sidewalk toward her house.

"I'd ask what their favorite food is and I'd tell it all about the greatest girl detective ever." He grinned.

"You would not!"

"I would!"

"You'd show them Magellan." She smiled.

"Yes, I probably would do that." Mouse unzipped Magellan's pouch and peered in at the tiny mouse. "You'd probably be about the same size as the aliens, Magellan. They might make you their king!"

"Magellan, king of the tiny aliens." Rebekah laughed. "Mouse, you always find a way to cheer me up."

"It's my job." He shrugged, then followed Rebekah into her house.

"Okay, I'll use my phone to look up info about the other school. You can use my computer to look up information about tiny aliens if you want to." She opened it up for him.

"Great. I'm sure I'll find something." Mouse sat down in front of the computer.

"It looks like the Leprechauns have a game tomorrow afternoon." Rebekah scrolled through the information on her phone. "I think I'll go check it out and see what they're up to."

"Good idea, because I'm getting nowhere on the tiny alien theory. There was one picture, but it turned out to be ants, not aliens. I did find this though." Mouse pointed to the screen. "Does that look like what you saw?"

"A little." Rebekah nodded.

"It's a spy drone." Mouse frowned. "You might be right about the Leprechauns."

FIVE

After school the next day, Rebekah's mother dropped her and Mouse off at the Leprechauns' soccer field.

"It looks like the game has already started." Rebekah walked toward the field. "If they are busy playing, I might be able to find where they are hiding that spy drone. Then we'll have proof of what they were doing. If they were cheating, they could get disqualified from playing this year."

"How are we going to find it, though?" Mouse looked around at the crowd of people on the bleachers. "There are so many people here. They probably don't have it out where someone can just see it."

"Exactly. We need to look near their bench and also keep an eye out for anyone acting suspicious." Rebekah made her way through the crowd toward the team's bench.

The crowd erupted in cheers as one of the players made a goal.

"Easy to do when you don't have a spy drone distracting you!" Rebekah huffed.

"It could still be a UFO, don't forget." Mouse smiled.

"No time for that right now, Mouse, we have to find the

drone." Rebekah crept up behind the team's bench and eyed a pile of towels. It looked like a good hiding spot to her. She picked up the corner of one towel and looked underneath.

"Maybe over there?" Mouse pointed to a table with a big cooler and refreshments. "There are some boxes underneath the table."

"Good eye. Let's take a look." Rebekah knelt down and peered under the table. She opened up one of the boxes and discovered a bunch of green and gold shirts. "Just some extra uniforms." She pulled open the second box and leaned under the table to get a better look. Inside was an assortment of supplies, from first aid to hair gel. She noticed something round at the bottom and dug through the supplies to get a better look.

"Just what do you think you're doing?" a voice called out from above the table.

Rebekah jumped and smacked herself on the bottom of the table. "Ouch." She rubbed her head as she backed out from under it.

A girl in a green and gold uniform placed her hands on her hips and glared at her. "You shouldn't be here. You're not on our team."

"And you shouldn't be using *this* to spy on my team!" Rebekah pulled the round item from the bottom of the box and held it up for the girl in front of her to see.

"What? Do you think I'm some kind of witch?" The girl stared at her.

Rebekah looked from the girl to the object she held in her hand. It was round, as she had seen, but it was also flat and had a reflective surface on the front.

"Do you think that's a magic mirror that lets me see your team play?"

SIX

"No, that's not what I thought!" Rebekah frowned as she dropped the mirror back into the box. "This might not be your drone, but I did see it yesterday while we were playing our first practice game!"

"I have no idea what you're talking about." The girl shook her head. "I don't have any drone. You're the only one spying around here. You're sneaking around by our team bench. That's cheating, you know! Your whole team could be disqualified because of it!"

"No, wait, that's not what I'm doing!" Rebekah crossed her arms. "I would never cheat! I am just trying to find out who was flying a drone over my soccer field yesterday."

"Sure, you're not cheating." The girl rolled her eyes. "You can believe what you want, but it wasn't us and I can prove it."

"How?" Mouse stepped forward.

"Here." She picked up a bag from beside the bench and pulled a phone out of it. "Look for yourself. The whole team was away at a game yesterday afternoon."

Rebekah stared at the pictures on the girl's phone. It was

clear that the team was at a game in another town at the time that Rebekah's team was practicing.

"That is pretty good proof." Rebekah handed the phone back. "I guess I was wrong, I'm sorry."

"We may want to win, but we don't have to cheat to do that." The girl shook her head. "We spend our time practicing, not sneaking around other team's benches." She turned and ran back onto the field.

"That didn't go well." Mouse frowned as he followed Rebekah back to the parking lot.

Rebekah finished sending a text to her mother and sighed. "Actually, it did. Maybe I was wrong, but at least now I know for sure that the Leprechauns weren't involved. It's not what I expected, but it does get us closer to solving the mystery."

"So, it might be aliens after all?" Mouse's eyes widened.

"Maybe." Rebekah waved as her mother pulled up. "I'm not sure yet. I think we need to go back to where this all started and have another look. I might have missed something."

She settled into the backseat with Mouse beside her. "Mom, do you mind dropping us off at school?"

"No problem, but you'll have to walk home after that, because I need to make dinner."

"Thanks." Rebekah looked out the window as they drove toward her school. Her hunch had been wrong, but she still knew that she had seen something, and she needed to find out exactly what it was.

"Don't worry, Rebekah." Mouse smiled as they arrived at their school. "We'll figure this out."

"Mouse!" Rebekah gasped as she climbed out of the car behind him.

"What?"

"Look up!" Rebekah pointed up at the sky.

A circular object darted through the clouds above them.

SEVEN

"It's back!" Rebekah gasped as she stared up at the flying object.

"I see it too!" Mouse grabbed her arm. "We have to catch it!"

"We can't fly!" Rebekah frowned as the object darted away from them in the sky. It hovered over the baseball field, where a game was being played.

"Do you think it's after them?" Mouse gulped. "We can't fly, but we can run! Let's see if we can catch up with it!"

Mouse took off running at full speed.

Rebekah ran after him. She tried to keep her eyes on the object while also watching out for the fans that crowded close to the baseball field.

"Look how high it's going!" Mouse pointed up at it as it climbed higher and higher in the sky.

"Can a drone even go that high?" Rebekah shielded her eyes as she looked up.

"A spy drone can, I bet." Mouse frowned. "It's moving away from the field."

"Let's see where it goes." Rebekah ran after it.

As it flew further from the field, a strong gust of wind blew through the area. Rebekah's hair flipped forward into her eyes.

As she pulled her hair back from her face, she saw the object flip and spin through the air. Another gust of wind pushed it hard toward the trees at the back of the field.

"Whatever it is, I think it's out of control!" Rebekah did her best to follow after it.

"It's headed right for that tree!" Mouse shouted over his shoulder. "Hopefully it won't vanish!"

"Not this time." Rebekah slowed down as she saw the object slam into the trunk of the tree, then catch on a few branches. "This time it's not going anywhere!"

"Oh no!" Mouse gasped as he ran toward the tree. "The tiny aliens! What if they're hurt?"

For an instant, Rebekah felt bad for the tiny aliens. Then she ran after Mouse. "Be careful, Mouse! We still don't know what it is!"

"I know it's probably not tiny aliens, but what if it is? I have to save them!" Mouse spun the pouch around his waist to his back. Then he started to climb the tree.

Rebekah stood below and watched as he got closer to the object. "Can you see what it is?"

"Almost!" Mouse climbed a little further. He stared at the object. Then he grabbed it and pulled it free of the branches. He held it up in the air as he leaned back to look at Rebekah. "No aliens! It's definitely a drone!"

Another gust of wind kicked up and blew through Mouse's hair and shirt. He clung to the tree and the drone.

"Mouse! Get down here!" Rebekah frowned. "It's not safe!"

Mouse made his way down the tree. Once both his feet were on the ground, he held the drone out to Rebekah.

"You were right." He pointed to the camera on the drone. "It's definitely a spy drone. Someone is watching our school!"

EIGHT

Rebekah stared at the tiny camera, then looked up at Mouse. "But this doesn't make any sense. Who would be spying on our soccer game if it wasn't the Leprechauns?"

"I'm not sure, but it was definitely someone." Mouse pointed to the camera again. "There's a chip in this. If we can see what's on it, it might give us a clue about who the spy is."

"Great!" Rebekah glanced toward the school. "The school's still open. I bet we can find what we need in the computer lab."

"So, what you're saying is you want to break into the computer lab?" Mouse cringed. "What do you think Mr. Cooper is going to think about that?"

"Mr. Cooper!" Rebekah's eyes widened. "I bet he's the one behind this! He's probably using drones to spy on all the students! You know how strange he is."

"We'd better hope not." Mouse gasped. "Because I don't think he's going to be very happy about us stealing his drone!"

"If we can get the chip loaded up on one of the computers, then we can delete any of the pictures with us on it." Rebekah started toward the school. "Hurry, we don't have much time."

"Rebekah!" Mouse jogged after her. "The thing about drones is that usually someone has to fly them! Someone is going to be looking for that drone!"

"I know, so we have to run!" Rebekah neared the front door of the school with the drone clutched in her hand. She wasn't sure what she would find on the chip inside of it, but she hoped that it would lead her to the truth.

She burst through the door and headed down the hall that led to the computer lab.

She heard Mouse's footsteps right behind her.

"Rebekah!" Mr. Cooper called out from one of the classrooms.

Rebekah skidded to a stop. Her heart pounded. Had he already caught her?

"No running!" He sighed as he looked from her to Mouse. "How many times do I have to say that?"

"Sorry, Mr. Cooper." Mouse stepped in front of Rebekah and tried to block the drone in her hand with his body. "We were just excited."

"It's great to be excited, kids, but running in the hallway can lead to serious injuries. Please be more careful."

"We will, Mr. Cooper." Rebekah forced a smile. "I promise."

"Good." He nodded, then stepped back into the classroom.

"Do you think he saw the drone?" Rebekah whispered to Mouse as they continued down the hall.

"If he did, he didn't seem to recognize it. Maybe it's not him after all." Mouse pushed open the door to the computer lab. "Let's find out who it belongs to before we get into even more trouble."

While Mouse pulled the chip out of the drone, Rebekah turned one of the computers on.

"It fits here." Mouse slid the chip into one of the slots on the computer. "What's on it?"

Rebekah hit a few buttons, then a file full of pictures opened up on the screen.

"Me." Rebekah's eyes widened. "I'm on it!"

"Ouch! Is that when you fell?" Mouse looked at the picture of Rebekah with both feet up in the air. "You do need to work on your kick!"

"Mouse." Rebekah glared at him. "It was because I was distracted!"

"Sorry." He smiled. "What else is on there? Is it all just you?"

"No, it's not." She began to flip through the pictures. "Actually, there's pictures of lots of different people, but they're all on the sports fields. See, here's the baseball players." She made one of the pictures larger. "This is from today."

"Why would anyone be spying on all of the sports teams?" Mouse shook his head. "It doesn't make any sense. Who would do that?"

"I'm not sure. It could still be Mr. Cooper, right?" Rebekah continued to look through the pictures. "He may want to make sure that we're not tearing up the new field."

"That's a lot of trouble just to keep an eye on the fields though. Don't you think the coaches would make sure the fields are taken care of?"

"I guess you're right." Rebekah sighed. "So now we know that it is a drone, and we know who the drone is taking pictures of, but we don't know who is flying the drone."

"Whoever was flying it is probably out looking for it." Mouse stood up. "We should go back out to the baseball field and see if anyone is looking."

"Great idea!" Rebekah took the chip out of the computer and tucked it back into the drone. "Whoever is doing this better have a good explanation."

As she stepped out into the hallway, she spotted Mr. Wiley, the janitor, headed their way. He was carrying a ladder. A girl walked beside him, and she was clearly upset.

"I'm telling you that I was being careful! I never would have flown it into a tree! But the wind caught it and sent it flying!"

"Sure, I hear you." Mr. Wiley sighed and lifted the ladder higher on his shoulder. "Just show me where it is. I'm sure that we can get it down."

Mouse stepped out into the hallway beside Rebekah with the drone in his hand.

"Hey!" The girl shouted as she charged toward him. "That's my drone!"

"Calm down, Annie!" Mr. Wiley huffed as the girl nearly knocked the ladder out of his grasp.

"Is it?" Mouse glanced at Rebekah, then stepped back.

"You're the one that's been flying this thing?" Rebekah crossed her arms. "I have a lot of questions for you!"

"So do I!" Annie put her hands on her hips. "Starting with, what are you doing with my drone?"

"I found it." Mouse frowned. "It was stuck in a tree."

"And you just decided that made it yours?" Annie shook her head. "It doesn't belong to you, and you know it!"

"So, we don't need the ladder then?" Mr. Wiley raised his eyebrows.

"No, Mr. Wiley, we don't need it. But we might need Mr. Cooper if this boy decides that he's not going to give me my drone back!"

TEN

"I'll give it back!" Mouse glared at her. "I'm not a thief!"

"But first you have to tell us why you were taking pictures of all of the sports teams!" Rebekah stepped in front of her. "Don't you know anything about respecting a person's privacy?"

"Excuse me, but I have permission to take pictures of the sports teams!"

Mr. Wiley shook his head as he walked off.

"You do?" Rebekah frowned. "Why?"

"I run the student newspaper and the website. I take pictures of the sports teams with the drone so that I can put them on the website, and I also put some of the pictures in the newspaper." She cringed as she looked at Rebekah. "And I'm guessing that you're a little upset because of what happened yesterday."

"What do you mean?" Rebekah narrowed her eyes.

"I felt so bad when I saw you fall. I realized that my drone must have startled you. I was too embarrassed to come over and ask if you were okay."

"I'm fine." Rebekah smiled. "Your drone did startle me, but I think it's great that you're running the newspaper. That must be so much fun!"

"Most of the time it is." She smiled. "I love investigating stories."

"Here you go." Mouse handed Annie the drone. "The chip is in there and the pictures are good."

"Great." Annie shook her head. "I'm on a deadline. I was so worried that the chip might have been damaged."

"So, you investigate lots of different things happening at our school?" Rebekah followed Annie into the computer lab.

"Yes, just about anything that happens here." She grinned as she looked at Rebekah. "That's how I already know that you're a detective!"

"You do?" Rebekah looked at Mouse, then back at Annie.

"Yup." She pointed to Mouse's pouch. "And I know all about Magellan too!"

"What?" Mouse gasped as he took a step back. "You're not going to tell Mr. Cooper, are you?"

"No, never." She frowned. "He's a little strange, isn't he?"

"We think so." Rebekah nodded. "Have you been inside of his office? Have you seen all of the strange things he has in there?"

"Yes!" Annie's eyes widened. "I asked him about them and he wouldn't tell me anything. When I tried to touch one of the statues--just to see how heavy it was--he snapped at me not to touch anything." She frowned. "Sometimes he seems pretty nice, letting me do whatever I want with the newspaper. But why does he have all that strange stuff in his office, and why can't I ask any questions about it?"

"That's what I'd like to know." Rebekah pulled her detective's notebook out of her backpack. "I've been keeping track of him."

"Me too." Annie raised an eyebrow. "If he does anything suspicious, I'll let you know."

"Thanks." Rebekah smiled.

She flipped open her notebook to the notes she'd made on the flying object mystery. She'd solved one mystery and maybe she'd gotten one step closer to solving the mystery of the very strange Mr. Cooper.

At the very least, she'd made a new friend and an ally.

BOOK 6: THE TERRIBLE SMELL

ONE

Mrs. Bilson clapped her hands as she walked in front of the line of students. "Let's go, get those knees up!"

Rebekah did her best to lift her knees higher. She knew that pumping them up and down would only strengthen her muscles and make her kicks in soccer even stronger.

As her heart pounded, sweat gathered on her forehead. Gym had not always been her favorite class at school. There was a time when she would do anything to avoid it, but now she looked forward to it as a chance to be active in the middle of the day.

"Carla, can you please participate?" Mrs. Bilson paused in front of one of the girls at the end of the line. "I know it can be hard to get started, but once you get going, you're going to enjoy it."

"I'm too tired." Carla covered her mouth as she yawned.

"Didn't you sleep last night?" Mrs. Bilson crossed her arms.

"Not well." Carla shook her head.

"Did the smell keep you awake?" A boy who stood beside Carla pinched his nose and shook his head.

"What smell?" Carla frowned.

"Nathan, remember to be kind." Mrs. Bilson clapped her hands. "Alright, everyone, take a break."

"Wait a minute, what smell?" Carla glared at Nathan.

Rebekah frowned. She hated to see anyone being teased and she knew that Nathan had a bad habit of teasing people.

"I don't know what you've been rolling around in, but you need to take a shower!" Nathan waved his hand in front of his nose.

"I took a shower this morning!" Carla put her hands on her hips. "I don't smell at all!"

"I smell it too!" Kelly spoke up from beside Nathan. "But it's not Carla, it's Nathan!" She scrunched up her nose. "Why are you trying to blame her when you're the smelly one?"

"Me?" Nathan gasped. "Are you kidding me? It's not me!"

"Enough!" Mrs. Bilson blew her whistle. "Being active can create certain smells. It's biological. It's perfectly natural. Good hygiene can help, but when you sweat and get active, you might experience some smells."

"Not this smell!" Arianna looked straight at Rebekah. "It's horrible and it's coming from Rebekah!"

Rebekah felt her cheeks go warm as all the kids looked at her. Her stomach twisted. Did she smell? She didn't think so. But everyone else did.

"It isn't me." She frowned. "I don't think so anyway." She sniffed the air. Her stomach flipped and lurched. "Oh, that's awful!" She stared at Arianna. She didn't want to make her feel bad, but she'd never smelled anything so terrible. "I have some extra clothes in my locker, Arianna. Do you want to borrow them?"

"What?" Arianna gasped. "It's not me!"

"Alright, that's it for class. Everyone get cleaned up and get changed." Mrs. Bilson pointed to the locker room.

Rebekah sniffed the air as her classmates walked past. Even though the smell was strong, it didn't seem to be coming from any one particular student.

TWO

While the other students headed into the locker rooms, Rebekah hung back. She continued to sniff the air. Even after all the other kids had left, the smell lingered just as strong.

Rebekah looked over at Mrs. Bilson, who was gathering equipment from the class. Could it be coming from her?

Mrs. Bilson walked to the other side of the gym.

The smell stayed right where it was.

"Oh no." Rebekah sighed. "Maybe it *is* me." She lifted one arm and took a sniff. It wasn't exactly pleasant, but it wasn't the smell that made her stomach lurch.

"If it's not me, and it's not any of the other kids or Mrs. Bilson, then where is that smell coming from?"

She thought about her detective's notebook tucked away in her backpack inside her gym locker. She wished she had it to start taking notes on the mystery she had stumbled across. Before she could get to it, she needed to see if she could find the source of the smell.

She walked around the gym slowly, sniffing the air with every step. In some places, the smell became stronger. In other places, the smell seemed to fade.

She began to trace a pattern of the stronger areas of the scent. As she followed it, it led toward a large bin near the entrance of the locker room. As she got closer to it, the smell increased.

It became so bad that she had to cover her nose. Her eyes began to water.

She peeked over the side of the large bin and saw piles of used towels.

"I guess that makes sense." She shuddered. "They would be pretty smelly." She started to dig through the towels. As she picked one up and lifted it to her nose, she prepared for the worst scent ever.

Instead, all she smelled was fabric and a bit of sweat.

She pulled the towel away from her nose and instantly smelled the horrible scent again.

"It's not the towels!" She dropped the towel back into the bin, then took a step back. She sniffed the air again. "Ugh! So gross!" She clapped her hand over her nose. She crouched down and sniffed again. "It's coming from under the bin." She grabbed the frame of the bin and gave it a push.

As the cart rolled away, Rebekah spotted a vent in the floor. A burst of the terrible scent blew up into her face.

"Yuck!" She stumbled back as she tried to get away from the smell. She coughed a few times and sucked down some fresh air. Then she looked back at the vent. "It's coming from the vent. It's coming from inside the school!"

"Rebekah!" Mrs. Bilson yelled to her from the other side of the gym. "I said go get cleaned up! If you have any questions about hygiene, we can always talk!"

Rebekah's cheeks burned again. "It's not me!"

She sighed and ran off to the locker room.

THREE

As Rebekah stepped inside the locker room, she heard all of the showers running. Near the lockers, girls were spraying on perfume and scented lotions. Rebekah guessed that every girl was trying to make sure that they weren't the source of the terrible smell.

Rebekah didn't bother. She knew that she wasn't the source of the smell.

After she changed out of her gym clothes, she grabbed her backpack out of her locker. She pulled her detective's notebook out of her backpack and flipped it open.

She began writing down notes about the smell and where she thought it might be coming from. She drew a sketch of the vent she'd found. Then she added a few questions underneath the sketch.

Where does the vent lead?

What might be inside of it that smells so bad?

"Maybe one of the towels got in there? Or maybe someone spilled their milk down the vent?"

She snapped the notebook shut. "Whatever is causing that smell, I'm going to find out."

She frowned as she left the locker room. But how would she get inside the vent?

She could ask Mr. Wiley, the janitor, for help, but she doubted that he would believe her.

"Rebekah, what's wrong?" Mouse walked up to her in the hallway. "You have that look in your eyes. Did you find a mystery?"

"I sure did." She sighed as she looked at her best friend. "But I'm not sure how I'm going to solve this one. It's inside the walls!"

"What?" Mouse's eyes widened. "What do you mean?"

"There's a very strange smell coming from the vent in the gym. I figured out where it is coming from, but I don't know what's causing it. I have to find out! All of the kids at gym class were accusing each other of being the source of the smell. But I know none of them are." She shook her head. "What I don't know is what *is* causing the smell."

"How bad is it?" Mouse pushed the door to the gym open and took a sniff. "Wow!" He jumped back. "That's terrible!"

"I know." Rebekah cringed.

"It reminds me of a stink bomb that I smelled once." Mouse scrunched up his nose. "It was the worst. I was at a party for my friend's birthday, and the person that set it off thought it was some big joke. But it wasn't! We all had to leave the house and my friend's mother had to get all of her furniture cleaned."

"Wow, that sounds awful. Who would do something like that at a birthday party?"

"Him!" Mouse pointed a finger at a boy who was running down the hall toward them. "Gus Baker!"

"What?" Gus skidded to a stop. "Why are you two looking at me like that?"

FOUR

"Gus." Mouse stared straight at him. "What have you been up to?"

"Me?" Gus frowned. "Lots of things. Can you narrow it down a bit?"

"Take a sniff." Rebekah pushed open the door to the gym.

"What?" He laughed. "You want me to sniff the gym?"

"Yes." Rebekah continued to hold the door open.

"Alright." Gus raised an eyebrow, then stepped forward and took a sniff. "Wow! Ugh! That's disgusting!"

"It smells like that stink bomb you set off." Mouse crossed his arms as Gus turned to look at him.

"You're right, it does actually." He shrugged. Then his eyes widened. "Oh, wait a minute, do you think I had something to do with this?" He shook his head. "No way! I didn't do anything!"

"Look, Gus, I like a prank as much as anyone else—you know that." Mouse frowned. "But this one is getting out of control. Whatever you did, we can help you fix it. You just have to tell us the truth."

"I didn't do anything!" Gus gasped. Then his eyes narrowed. "You're trying to get me into trouble, aren't you?"

"Of course not. Why would I do that?" Mouse shook his head. "We just want to get rid of the smell."

"Well, I didn't do it, and if you tell anyone I did, I'll tell Mr. Cooper about Magellan!" He pointed to the pouch that Mouse wore around his waist.

"You wouldn't!" Mouse gasped. "If he finds out, I won't be allowed to bring Magellan to school anymore! He gets so sad when he's home alone."

"I won't say a word unless you tell Mr. Cooper I had something to do with this." He crossed his arms as he looked over at Rebekah. "I thought you were supposed to be a good detective. Can't you tell that I'm telling the truth?"

Rebekah frowned. She wasn't sure what to believe. Gus could easily be lying. If he'd planted a stink bomb once, she guessed that he would do it again.

"I'll get to the truth, Gus. There's no doubt about that." Rebekah looked into his eyes. "Not a word about Magellan, understand?"

"Sure, I won't say anything—as long as I don't end up in Mr. Cooper's office." Gus turned and walked off down the hall.

"What are we going to do?" Mouse frowned. "If it was Gus who did this, I know he'll tell Mr. Cooper about Magellan."

"We don't know that it was him." Rebekah glanced back at the gym door. "He did seem very surprised by the smell."

"He could have been pretending." Mouse unzipped Magellan's pouch and reached in to pet the mouse. "Don't worry, Magellan, you're not going to get stuck at home all day."

"We can't know for sure if Gus did this or not unless we find more proof. We have to figure out what's inside that vent. But how are we going to do that?" Rebekah shook her head. "They're too small for us to fit into."

"I have an idea." Mouse smiled. "Meet me at the computer lab after school, okay?"

"I'll be there." Rebekah nodded.

FIVE

Rebekah spent most of her day looking over the notes in her detective's notebook. She tried to think of things that might make the kind of smell that was coming from the vent. She drew pictures of what she thought it might be.

One picture was a trash can. Another was a piece of rotten fruit.

She did her best to describe the smell as well. Maybe if she could figure out what the smell was, she could figure out where it might be coming from.

After the last bell rang, she headed for the computer lab and found Mouse already there with their friend Annie.

They stood close together and leaned over a box on a table.

"Mouse? Annie? What are you doing?"

"Just a second." Annie glanced up at her, then looked back into the box. "Is it working now, Mouse?"

Mouse looked at his phone, then nodded. "Yes, it's much clearer now."

"What is?" Rebekah tried to peer over his shoulder. Impatient to find out what they were up to, she peeked over the side of the box. "Magellan? What are you wearing?"

"Shh!" Mouse looked toward the door, then back at her. "We don't want to draw anyone's attention, especially Mr. Cooper's."

'I'm sorry." She nodded. "But what does Magellan have strapped to his back?"

"It's a camera." Annie smiled proudly. "I was able to get it out of my drone and attach it to Magellan with a strap. Now he can be a little mouse drone."

"You're going to send Magellan into the vent?" Rebekah's eyes widened. "And you can see everything he sees on your phone?"

"Yes, isn't it great?" Mouse grinned. "Magellan, the superhero."

"Thanks so much for helping, Annie." Rebekah smiled at her.

"Oh, I don't mind at all. This is going to make a great story for the school newspaper. Mouse said I can print whatever you two find out."

"Did he?" Rebekah raised an eyebrow.

"With a smell like that, it has to be a great story. Annie will do a good job with her article." Mouse scooped Magellan up out of the box.

"I'm sure you're right about that." Rebekah smiled. "Alright, we'll make sure we get all the details for you."

"Thanks." Annie frowned. "But—uh—if you should get caught, maybe don't mention my help?"

"Not a word." Rebekah nodded. "Let's go find out what's smelling up our school." Rebekah led the way from the computer lab to the gym.

Mouse kept Magellan hidden in his hands as he watched for any sign of Mr. Cooper.

Rebekah looked up and down the hall, then pushed open the door to the gym.

The smell wafted right into her nostrils.

"Ugh! Maybe we should give Magellan nose plugs!"

"He'll be okay." Mouse smiled as he looked into his pet's eyes. "He's a brave little mouse."

SIX

Rebekah pried open the vent on the floor of the gym.

Mouse crouched down and set Magellan inside of the vent.

"Alright, boy, make sure you find that smell, okay?" He pulled out his phone and turned it on.

Magellan looked up at him, wiggled his nose, then took off in the vent.

"Do you really think he'll know what to look for?" Rebekah peered inside.

"Maybe not, but he'll probably run into it at some point." Mouse stood up. "The camera will let me see where he is too, so we can follow him." He pointed to the door. "He's already headed down the hallway, and I haven't seen anything strange on the video yet."

"Let's try to keep up with him." Rebekah pushed open the door of the gym and almost walked into Mr. Wiley.

"Kids, you shouldn't be in there." He shook his head. "There's a terrible smell, and we're not sure what it is yet."

"We're just leaving." Rebekah gulped as she glanced at Mouse. Would Mr. Wiley see the open vent? "But we're pretty sure the smell is coming from the cafeteria. I smelled it in there earlier. I know it's stronger in the gym, but I think it starts in the cafeteria."

"Oh yeah?" Mr. Wiley frowned. "I guess that would make sense. I'll go check it out. Thanks, kids." He turned his cart around and pushed it toward the cafeteria.

"Good thinking, Rebekah!" Mouse looked down at his phone. "Magellan is way ahead of us now, though."

"Don't worry, we'll catch up. Just give me a second!" Rebekah ran back into the gym. She grabbed the bin full of towels and rolled it over the open vent. Then she ran back to Mouse in the hallway. "Ugh, I think the smell is getting worse. It's terrible!"

"I know, it's making me sick to my stomach." He held up his phone. "Magellan reached the end of the vent."

"And there was nothing there?" Rebekah's eyes widened.

"Nothing that I saw. But maybe I missed something." He frowned as he scrolled back through the video feed.

"Let's find out where he is at least. Maybe that will tell us something."

"This way." Mouse led the way down the hall and around a corner. When he looked up from his phone again, they stood right in front of Mr. Cooper's office.

"The vent leads here?" Rebekah sniffed the air. "It does smell a bit like the gym, just not as strong."

"You're right." Mouse shook his head. "But there was nothing in the vent. Not that I can see in the video, anyway."

"So maybe the smell is coming from Mr. Cooper's office and wafting through the vent." Rebekah narrowed her eyes. "We know that Mr. Cooper is strange and keeps weird statues and old books in his office. Maybe he's added something new to his collection."

"Something smelly?" Mouse cringed. "What could smell that bad?"

Rebekah thought about it for a moment, then she took a sharp breath.

"Something old—very old. Like a mummy!"

SEVEN

"A mummy?" Mouse's eyebrows raised. "You think Principal Cooper has a mummy in his office?"

"Well, maybe not a mummy, but something like one." Rebekah shrugged. "It wouldn't surprise me if he did. He has such a strange collection of things, and he won't tell anyone about them or let anyone touch them!" Rebekah shook her head. "Something's definitely not right there."

"You might be right." Mouse shivered. "I don't want to go to school with a mummy."

"None of us do." Rebekah narrowed her eyes. "And we're not going to. We just have to get inside that office."

"How are we going to do that?" Mouse reached for the knob and gave it a twist. "It's locked. I figured it would be."

"Mr. Cooper keeps the door locked when he's not in there." Rebekah glanced up and down the hall. "I don't see any sign of him, which probably means that he can't stand the smell in there either. We need to keep him away long enough to get inside. We also need his key."

"First, we need to get Magellan back, right?" Mouse met her eyes.

"Of course. But if we can't get inside Mr. Cooper's office, then we'll have to get him out back in the gym. Do you think he'll come back to you?"

"Definitely. I have his favorite snack." Mouse pulled a few pieces of cheese out of his pocket.

"Great, you get Magellan safe, and I'll find Mr. Cooper."

Rebekah walked down the hallway in the direction of the front of the school. "If I were a principal where would I be?"

She passed the front door and found no sign of him. She walked through the cafeteria, toward the door that led out onto the playground.

"Rebekah!" Mr. Wiley called out. "Come here!"

Rebekah frowned. She turned around as Mr. Wiley stepped out of the kitchen, followed by Mr. Cooper.

"There she is. She's the one that told me the smell was coming from here," said Mr. Wiley.

"Rebekah, why did you tell Mr. Wiley that?" Mr. Cooper crossed his arms. "This is a very serious matter."

"I was confused." Rebekah shrugged. "I came to get you, because the smell is even worse in the gym. I thought you might want to check it out again."

"That's where we're headed." Mr. Cooper walked toward the door, then looked back at her. "You can come along with us."

Rebekah stared at him as he held the door open. Yes, her principal was strange. She had a whole file on him in her detective's notebook, but would he really keep a mummy in his office?

"Sure!" She smiled as she followed after them.

Hopefully, Mouse had already gotten Magellan out of the vent.

When they stepped into the gym, Mouse had just zipped up Magellan's pouch.

"Mouse!" Rebekah waved to him. "Mr. Cooper and Mr. Wiley are here to investigate the smell."

"Oh, great!" Mouse smiled. "I know where it's coming from!"

EIGHT

"You do?" Mr. Cooper raised an eyebrow.

"You do?" Rebekah's eyes widened.

"Mr. Cooper, do you have a key to the storage room by the locker room?" Mouse nudged the towel bin back over the vent.

Rebekah guessed that he hadn't put the cover back on yet. She also guessed, from the way he looked at her, that he hadn't solved the mystery after all.

"Sure I do, let's have a look." Mr. Cooper pulled his keys out of his pocket. Rebekah watched as he unlocked the door to the storage room.

Just as he slipped his keys back into his pocket, she lurched forward and bumped into his side. She snatched the key ring before it could slip into his pocket.

"Rebekah, are you okay?" Mr. Cooper helped her straighten up.

"I'm sorry, the smell in here, it's just too much for me."

"It's too much for all of us." Mr. Cooper nodded. "But don't worry, we're taking care of it. Why don't you go outside? Mouse can show us what he found."

"Thanks, yes, I'll do that." Rebekah turned and hurried out of the gym back into the hallway.

With the keys clasped tightly in her hand, her heart pounded. She knew that if Mr. Cooper figured out that she had taken them, she'd be in serious trouble. But she also knew that her school couldn't go on with such a terrible smell.

She sorted through the keys on the ring and found a few that might fit the lock. As she tried the first one, she glanced around, hoping not to get spotted.

"It doesn't fit!" She frowned, then tried the next one.

She smiled with relief as the knob turned. She pushed open the door.

The smell smacked her right in the nose. She could barely take a breath. She covered her nose and breathed through her mouth instead. As she stepped further into the room, the door swung shut behind her.

On the shelves all over the walls, eerie statues and old stone faces stared down at her. On the bookshelves behind Mr. Cooper's desk, there were ancient books with strange symbols and letters. In display cases not far from his desk were an assortment of stones, gems, and small broken tools.

She'd never seen so many strange and old things in one place before.

On his desk, she spotted a book with notes about the different items in the office.

"What are you up to, Mr. Cooper?" She sighed as she ran her fingertips over one of the display cases. She could see the latch on it was unlocked.

It would be easy enough to open it up and have a closer look at the items, but that wasn't what she was there to do. She had another mystery to solve.

"If I were a mummy where would I be?" Rebekah pulled

open the door to the only closet in the room. As she did, some-thing long and thin fell toward her.

She gasped as she saw finger bones curl around her shoulder.

NINE

A scream erupted from Rebekah's mouth just as the door to the principal's office swung open.

"Rebekah! What are you doing in here?"

Mr. Cooper glared at her as Mouse ran into the room behind him.

"It's got me!" Rebekah gulped as she stumbled away from the bony grasp.

"Rebekah." Mr. Cooper sighed, then pulled the hand off her shoulder. "It's just an extra skeleton from the science room. It's not going to hurt you." He tucked the skeleton back into the closet, then closed the door. When he turned to face her, his eyes narrowed. "Now answer my question. What are you doing in here?

"I was just—uh." Rebekah gasped.

"Just tell him the truth, Rebekah." Mouse frowned. "There's no point in hiding it now." He looked up at Mr. Cooper. "We figured out that the smell was coming from your office, and we didn't want to hurt your feelings."

"What?" Mr. Cooper frowned. "How did you figure that out?"

Mouse put his hands over Magellan's pouch.

"Detective work." Rebekah cleared her throat. "We didn't want to embarrass you, but we wanted to figure out where the smell was coming from." She held out his keys. "Sorry, Mr. Cooper."

He snatched the keys from Rebekah's hand. "I keep my office locked for a reason. Understand?"

"Yes." Rebekah glanced at all of the strange items, then looked back at him. "We're sorry, we'll just be going."

"Oh no you don't." He stepped in front of the door. "You two are not going anywhere until you tell me where that smell is coming from. It's driving me crazy!"

"Oh, well..." Rebekah's heart pounded as she realized she didn't have an answer for him. But she needed to get one and fast.

She took another look around the room and spotted the vent that Magellan had found. She looked up from the vent and saw a window right above it. The curtains swirled around as a breeze carried through the window.

"Oh!" She covered her nose, then nodded. "That's it! It's coming from outside!" She walked over to the window, then pulled the curtains back. "Mr. Cooper, there is a vent right under this window. So when the wind blows, all of the smell from outside goes down into the vent and it comes out inside the gym."

"Good work, Rebekah." Mr. Cooper peered out through the window. "But what could be outside that smells like that? It's just awful."

"I think I might have an idea." Rebekah smiled as she thought about the things she'd drawn in her notebook over the past few weeks.

TEN

Rebekah led Principal Cooper and Mouse outside the school. She walked across the sports fields toward a large dome.

"This is the garden club's greenhouse, right?"

"Yes, it is." Mr. Cooper frowned as they got close to it. "Oh, I can smell it now! That's where it's coming from!"

"How could flowers and plants make that kind of smell?" Mouse gagged.

"They shouldn't." Mr. Cooper crossed his arms. "Something isn't right here."

"I think it might be this." Rebekah pinched her nose as she walked toward a hole dug not too far from the greenhouse. "It's a compost heap, isn't it?"

"Yes, I believe so." Mr. Cooper's voice came out strange as he pinched his nose as well.

"Ugh!" Mouse shook his head. "Something is terribly wrong! Rebekah, how did you figure this out?"

"The smell reminded me of rotten fruit and trash. Once I realized the smell was coming from outside the window, I thought about the compost heap. I saw them making it during soccer practice. I guess when the wind blows, it comes in Mr.

Cooper's window and goes through the vent into the gym." She shook her head. "But it really shouldn't smell like this."

"You're right, it shouldn't. Something must have gone in there that shouldn't have. I'll speak with the garden club advisor so we can get this straightened out right away. In the meantime, I'll make sure all of the windows in the school are closed." Mr. Cooper turned to face Rebekah. "You did a great job, Rebekah. You really are a good little detective."

"Thank you, Mr. Cooper." Rebekah squeaked out her words as she kept her nose pinched.

"But we do still need to talk about you stealing my key and sneaking into my office." He sighed. "But let's talk about it somewhere a little less smelly." He walked back toward the school.

Rebekah and Mouse hung back a few steps and whispered to each other.

"We're going to get detention for a year." Mouse frowned.

"Not you. Me! I'm the one who broke in, remember?" She shrugged. "But it was worth it. Now we solved the mystery of the smelly gym, and we also know a little bit more about what Mr. Cooper has in his office."

"I hope you still think it's worth it when he tells you what you're in for." Mouse shook his head.

"Alright, kids, in my office." Mr. Cooper opened the door to the school.

"Mr. Cooper, Mouse really didn't do anything wrong, did he?" Rebekah shrugged.

"Oh, you think I don't know that whenever one of you is up to something, both of you are involved?" He opened his office door. "Let's go."

Rebekah frowned as she stepped inside.

Mr. Cooper walked over to the window and closed it. "Hopefully, it won't take too long to get rid of that smell." He turned around to look at them. "As for you two, I'm really disappointed."

"We're sorry, Mr. Cooper." Mouse sighed. "Really we are."

"I'm disappointed that you two still don't think you can come to me instead of sneaking around." He looked straight at Rebekah. "You're such a good detective. Can't you tell that I am someone you can trust?"

Rebekah frowned. In his office, surrounded by his strange collection, she had no idea what to expect from him.

"Maybe you could tell me a little bit about your collection?" She reached for one of the statues.

"Don't touch that!" He sighed. "Both of you may go. There won't be any detention this time. I hope that next time you have questions, you'll come to me for help."

"We will." Mouse nodded, then hurried Rebekah out of the office. "Maybe he isn't so bad after all."

"Maybe." Rebekah glanced back as Mr. Cooper closed the door. "But he is one mystery I'm determined to solve."

BOOK 7: THE MISSING NOTEBOOK

ONE

Rebekah walked quickly toward the front door of the school with her best friend, Mouse, trailing behind her.

"The new girl arrives today, doesn't she?" Mouse tried to catch up with Rebekah.

"Yes, I can't wait." Rebekah smiled. "She just moved here from Mexico, and I get to show her around."

"It was nice of Mr. Cooper to ask you to do that." Mouse sighed. "Rebekah, can you please slow down?"

"Sorry." Rebekah slowed down as she looked over at her best friend. "I'm just excited. I want to show her everything I can so that she feels more comfortable here."

"I'm sure you'll do a great job." Mouse unzipped the pouch around his waist and peeked in at the mouse inside. "Do you think I should introduce her to Magellan? Or do you think she'll tell Mr. Cooper?"

"Let me talk to her a bit first. I'm going to find out everything about her."

"Oh, she's your newest mystery, huh?" Mouse grinned. "Rebekah, girl detective, investigates new girl. You don't think she's a spy, do you?"

"No!" Rebekah laughed. "But I am very curious about her. All I know so far is that her name is Camila and she is from Mexico."

As they reached the school, Rebekah saw a crowd of kids headed inside. She wondered if one of them might be Camila.

"See you at lunch, Rebekah!" Mouse waved to her, then took off into the crowd.

She made her way through the other students and then headed for the main office. She spotted a girl sitting alone inside.

"Camila?" Rebekah smiled as she poked her head inside.

The girl looked up at her with a small smile. "Rebekah?"

"That's me!" Rebekah grinned and stepped inside the office. "I've been looking forward to meeting you."

"Me too." Camila grabbed her backpack.

"I have so much to show you." Rebekah grabbed Camila's hand and pulled her out of the office.

"This school is huge!" Camila sighed. "I'm sure I'll get lost!"

"Not a chance." Rebekah smiled. "I'll show you everything you need to know. It is big, but once you know a few tricks it'll be much easier to find where things are. Like this section here." She gestured to the hall to the right of them. "It's the science and history section. The school is broken up by subject to make things a little easier to remember."

"Oh, that's great." Camila nodded.

"So Camila, what's your favorite thing to do back home?" Rebekah pointed out the water fountain and the bathrooms.

"I like to read." Camila shrugged.

"Oh, any favorite books?" Rebekah smiled as she pointed out the library. "I'm sure you can find things you'll like in there."

"Great, thanks. Sometimes I like to read mystery books."

"Oh, I like mysteries too." Rebekah glanced up at the clock. "We'd better get to our first class."

As she walked with Camila toward the classroom, she couldn't help but be curious about the girl. So far she hadn't said too much, but Rebekah guessed that she might be a little nervous. By lunch, she was sure they would be good friends.

TWO

By lunchtime, other than the fact that Camila enjoyed reading mysteries, Rebekah hadn't found a lot in common with the new girl. While Rebekah loved playing soccer, Camila didn't like to play any sports. Rebekah liked to listen to music and dance, while Camila preferred to play music on her piano and sing along.

Even getting those answers out of her was proving difficult, as Camila didn't seem to like to talk much. But then again, Rebekah had to admire her because she knew that Camila was used to speaking in Spanish.

Rebekah hoped that meeting Mouse would get her to be a little more lively.

"My best friend, Mouse, will eat lunch with us." Rebekah pushed open the door to the cafeteria. "You'll like him, he's really funny."

"Mouse?" Camila stared at her. "Is that really his name?"

"No, it's not. But that's what everyone calls him." She smiled. "He really likes mice. He has quite a few as pets."

"Mice?" Camila gasped. "How weird!"

"They're really sweet, actually, especially his favorite one, Magellan. Maybe you'd like to meet him?"

"Meet a mouse?" Camila shook her head. "I don't think so. I don't even like cats."

Rebekah's eyes widened. Who didn't like cats?

"Mouse!" She waved to him and led Camila over to their table. "Keep Magellan to yourself," she whispered.

"Okay." Mouse nodded, then smiled at Camila. "It's so nice to meet you, Camila."

"You too. Mouse?" Camila raised an eyebrow.

"That's my name." He grinned.

After they picked up their lunches, Mouse nudged Rebekah's elbow on the way back to the table.

"Can I talk to you for a second? Alone?"

"Sure." Rebekah smiled at Camila. "We'll be right there." She turned her attention to Mouse. "What is it?"

"Remember those weird deliveries that Mr. Cooper is getting?"

"Yes, you said you've seen boxes of different sizes delivered to his office every day this week." Rebekah frowned. "I've been keeping track of them in my notebook."

"He got another one this morning. A big one. Tall and skinny." He shrugged. "I don't know what was inside, but it just seems strange, doesn't it?"

"Yes, it does." Rebekah noticed Camila watching them from a few steps away.

"What are you two talking about?" She smiled.

"Oh, nothing." Mouse shrugged.

"Nothing important." Rebekah sat down at the table.

"Oh, okay." Camila frowned as she sat down as well.

For the rest of lunch, Camila barely said a word. She picked at her food and didn't laugh at any of Mouse's jokes.

"Camila, are you okay?" Rebekah looked into her eyes. "I

know all of this can feel pretty strange—being in a new school, in a new place, speaking a different language."

"I'm fine." Camila sighed. "I just wonder, does anything strange ever happen around here?"

"Strange?" Rebekah grinned.

"Yes, you know. Maybe, something unexplained?"

"Sometimes." Rebekah nodded. "But I always get it figured out."

"You do?" Camila smiled. "That must be fun."

"It is." Rebekah nodded. "Do strange things happen at your school?"

"Oh, you would not believe me if I told you!" Camila laughed.

Rebekah smiled. Maybe she and Camila had more in common than she thought.

THREE

After lunch at history class, Rebekah decided to make some notes about what Mouse had told her. She'd been keeping a close eye on their principal, Mr. Cooper, and these deliveries were just the latest in a string of strange things about him.

She pulled out her detective's notebook and flipped it open on her desk. After writing down a few notes, she glanced up to see Camila staring straight at her.

"Are those your notes?" Camila smiled. "Could I see them? Then I might have an idea about what's happening in this class."

"Oh no, these are different notes." Rebekah flipped the notebook shut.

"Rebekah." The girl in the desk in front of her turned around to look at her. "I have a case for you."

"Tell me more, Gabby!" Rebekah opened her notebook back up.

"I lost my saxophone."

"How did you lose a saxophone?" Rebekah's eyes widened. "It's so big."

"I know." Gabby sighed. "That's what my mother said too.

I'm just not sure where I left it. I thought it was at home, but it wasn't."

"Have you checked the music room?" Rebekah jotted down a note in her notebook.

"Yes, of course. But it wasn't there."

"Hmm." Rebekah tapped her pen against her lips. "What about the bus? Did you leave it on the bus?"

"No, I checked this morning." Gabby frowned. "You don't think someone took it, do you?"

"It's possible." Rebekah scanned the room. "Has anyone taken an interest in your saxophone?"

"It's in the gym!" Camila blurted out the words as she looked at them.

"What?" Rebekah blinked. "How do you know?"

"Oh, you're right!" Gabby smacked her forehead. "I left it in one of the big lockers in the gym because I forgot to leave it in the music room! Thank you so much. Camila, is it?" She smiled. "Rebekah, it looks like you might have some competition in the detective department."

Rebekah stared at Camila, who looked down at her own notebook. "How did you know that?"

"I noticed it when we were at gym class." Camila shrugged. "Sometimes I notice things like that."

"Good job." Rebekah smiled. "You solved your first mystery!"

"Sure, thanks." Camila smiled, then glanced up at Rebekah. "Is that what your notebook is for? Solving mysteries?"

"It's a special detective's notebook." Rebekah nodded. "I keep all the notes about my cases in it."

"That's clever. It's a good way to keep track of things." Camila stood up as the bell rang.

"Thanks again, Camila!" Gabby waved to her as she ran out of the classroom.

Rebekah walked behind Camila out into the hall. She was glad that Camila had solved Gabby's mystery, but she suspected there was a lot about Camila that she didn't know yet. Was she just pretending to be shy and quiet? She definitely seemed to pay close attention to details. Rebekah hadn't even noticed the saxophone in the gym locker room.

She decided she needed to find out more about Camila.

FOUR

"Let me walk you home." Rebekah led Camila down the sidewalk away from the school. "Do you like your new house?"

"Yes, it's nice. But we won't be here too long. My father is here for work for the rest of the year, then we'll be going back to our house in Mexico." Camila glanced around as she walked with Rebekah. "Do you like it here?"

"Very much. It's a small town, but it's full of nice people." Rebekah smiled. "I can show you the playground and the lake and there is a great spot in the woods where you can see deer and other animals."

"That would be great!" Camila grinned. "Thanks for showing me around today, Rebekah."

"Sure, I had fun. Would you like to come to dinner at my house the day after tomorrow? I can invite Mouse too."

"As long as he doesn't bring any of his pets." Camila laughed.

Rebekah smiled and did her best not to mention Magellan. "I'll tell him. How did you like the classes today?"

"They were interesting. We're studying a lot of the same

things." She paused in front of a small house. "This is it. See you tomorrow, Rebekah."

"Maybe I could come inside and we could go over the homework?" Rebekah glanced toward the house. She guessed that she could find out a lot more about Camila by seeing some of her things.

"Not today. I have a lot to unpack still. Maybe later this week?" Camila started toward the house.

"Sure, sounds good." Rebekah waved to her as Camila hurried into the house. She wondered if Camila was trying to get away from her. She'd done her best to be friendly to her, but she'd noticed throughout the day that Camila still didn't say much.

Rebekah continued down the sidewalk toward her house. Maybe Camila just didn't like her much? The thought made her a little sad. But she also wondered if Camila just didn't like all of the questions that Rebekah asked.

If Camila did have something to hide, she wouldn't want to have to answer so many questions.

Rebekah stepped into her house and called out to her mother. "I'm home, Mom! Can we have Mouse and another friend over for dinner the day after tomorrow?"

"Sure." Her mother stepped out of the kitchen and smiled at her. "Is it Camila? The new girl?"

"Yes." Rebekah flopped down on the sofa.

"That's great, I knew you two would get along."

"I'm not so sure about that." Rebekah sighed. "I don't think she likes me too much."

"Give her a little time. I'm sure it's strange to be in a new country and a new school. And she might be a little shy about speaking English."

"You're probably right. Oh, and her English is great—really impressive, actually." Rebekah unzipped her backpack and reached inside for her detective's notebook. She wanted to make a few notes about Camila. "Where is it?" She pulled all of her books out of her backpack, then turned it upside down and shook it. Her heart pounded as nothing fell out.

"Oh no!" She gasped. "My detective's notebook is gone!"

FIVE

"Mouse!" Rebekah burst through his back door and into his kitchen, where she knew he'd be having his after school snack.

"Rebekah!" Mouse dropped the piece of cheese he'd been feeding Magellan. "What's wrong?"

"My detective's notebook!" Rebekah gasped. "It's gone!"

"What do you mean it's gone?" Mouse frowned.

"I mean that it's not in my backpack where I put it!"

"Maybe you left it in your locker?" Mouse slid Magellan into his pouch and zipped it up.

"No way. I never leave my notebook at school. You know that if Mr. Cooper finds it, he'll see all of the notes that I've made about him." She groaned. "Oh no! What if he's already found it?"

"Just take a breath." Mouse stood up. "I'm sure that you just left it somewhere by accident—which means that you can still find it before anyone else does."

"How?" Rebekah sighed. "The school is already locked up for the day. There's no way I can get back in. Maybe with Mr. Wiley's help I could, but I don't think he'd help me."

"If the school is locked up, then that means no one else is there, right?" Mouse smiled. "So, no one else can find it. I'm sure if Mr. Wiley finds it, he'll put it in the lost and found and you can look there right away tomorrow."

"I can't believe I don't know where it is! Mouse, I would never just leave it somewhere, you know that."

"Yes, but today was a little strange. You had Camila to show around. Maybe you were distracted and just forgot to pick it up. Did you use it today?"

"Only to make notes about Mr. Cooper and the deliveries you told me about." She shook her head. "I didn't use it for anything else. I was going to make some notes about Camila this afternoon and that's when I realized it was missing."

"Notes about Camila? You think there's a mystery there?" Mouse narrowed his eyes. "What is it?"

"I'm not sure yet. She just seems to be hiding something." Rebekah shook her head. "That doesn't matter now. All that matters is finding my notebook before Mr. Cooper gets his hands on it."

"Well, I hate to say this, but what if you didn't lose it?" Mouse sat back down in his chair hard.

"What do you mean?"

"I mean, what if someone took it?" Mouse's eyes widened. "Someone who knows that we've been investigating him?"

"You mean Principal Cooper?" Rebekah gasped. "You think he might have stolen my notebook?"

"You said you never lose track of it. Who else would want to steal it? He's the only one you're investigating right now." Mouse frowned. "I'd hate to think that he would steal it, but I do think we have to consider it."

"If he did steal it, then we're going to be in big trouble." Rebekah slumped down in the chair next to him.

REBEKAH - GIRL DETECTIVE FIFTH GRADE MYSTERIES

"Tomorrow, retrace your steps and look everywhere. If it doesn't turn up, then we might have a problem." Mouse frowned.

223

SIX

At school the next day, Rebekah nearly left Camila behind as she rushed inside.

"Rebekah, wait for me!" Camila gasped as she ran after her. "I don't know how to get to all my classes yet."

"I'm sorry." Rebekah frowned. "I've got to hurry." As she met Camila's eyes, she thought about the last time she'd used her detective's notebook. "History class!" She turned and ran down the hall.

Camila followed after her. "Rebekah, what is going on?" She caught up with her at the door to the classroom. "What are you so upset about?"

"My detective's notebook." Rebekah looked through each desk, in the trash can, and even under the teacher's desk. "It's missing, and I have to find it."

"Maybe you left it at home?" Camila shrugged. "It's just a notebook."

"No!" Rebekah turned toward her. "It's not just a notebook! It's full of important information, and if it gets into the wrong hands, it could cause a lot of trouble!"

"Oh dear." Camila frowned. "I'm sorry. I hope you find it."

"I will. I have to." Rebekah sighed as the bell rang. "But first, we have to get to class."

She hurried Camila back down the hall to their first class of the day.

As she settled at her desk, her mind whirled with all the places her notebook might be. Had she thrown it out somehow? Left it on the soccer field?

She couldn't pay attention to a single thing that the teacher said.

Camila poked her arm. "Rebekah, someone's staring at you." She nodded toward the door.

Rebekah's eyes widened as she caught sight of Mr. Cooper, who was standing just inside the classroom door. And he was looking straight at her.

Rebekah braced herself for the moment he would call out her name.

Instead, he turned and walked back into the hallway.

Her heart pounded. Was he looking at her because he'd found her notebook? Did he want to discuss all of the things she'd written about him and his strange activities?

"Are you okay?" Camila frowned.

"I'll be fine. I think." Rebekah jumped as the bell rang. "Once I find my notebook."

At lunch, Rebekah pulled Mouse to the side and told him about Mr. Cooper's visit to her classroom.

"He came to mine too!" Mouse cringed. "He didn't say anything. He just looked at me and then left."

"I'm sure he has my notebook!" Rebekah sighed. "Why else would he be spying on us?"

"I don't know." Mouse shook his head.

"We have to get in his office and see if he has it. At least then we will know what to expect." She frowned.

"It's not going to be easy to get in there. He keeps it locked."

Mouse glanced over at Camila. "Maybe we should ask Camila to help."

"No way." Rebekah crossed her arms. "I'm not sure if I trust her yet."

"Didn't she help Gabby find her saxophone?"

Camila waved at them from their table.

"She did." Rebekah frowned. "But I don't want to risk getting her in trouble. Meet me after school by Mr. Cooper's office."

"Sure, I'll be there."

SEVEN

"Do you want to come to my house this afternoon?" Camila packed her books into her backpack as the bell rang for the last class of the day.

"I can't today. I have something I have to do with Mouse." Rebekah slung her backpack over her shoulder.

"Oh great, maybe I can tag along?" Camila smiled.

"Actually, there's a club I thought you might like. You said you like to play piano, right?" Rebekah led her down the hall toward the music room.

"Yes, I do!"

"Great. The music club is meeting. Gabby is part of it. Remember the girl whose saxophone you helped find?" She smiled.

"Sure, I remember."

"Great. She said you can join in this afternoon. I'm not a musician, so it's not really my thing, but I thought you'd enjoy it." Rebekah held her breath as she hoped that Camila would agree. She didn't want to hurt her feelings by telling her that she couldn't spend time with her and Mouse, but she also couldn't have her around when they tried to break into the principal's office.

"Okay, sounds good. Thanks, Rebekah." Camila looked at her. "What are you and Mouse doing?"

"Oh, just a little project, nothing very interesting." Rebekah waved to her as she walked away.

She spotted Mouse near Mr. Cooper's office.

"He's not in there right now." Mouse frowned. "But we have no way to get in."

"Maybe we can get him to go inside somehow?" Rebekah glanced around. "If we set Magellan loose, I'm sure that would get a lot of attention."

"You're right." Mouse started to unzip Magellan's pouch.

"Rebekah, Mouse—just who I was looking for." Mr. Cooper's hands came down on each of their shoulders. "Do you have a few minutes to talk?"

Rebekah's heart sank. She hadn't even noticed Mr. Cooper walk up behind them. Was she really such a great detective?

"Sure, Mr. Cooper." She followed him to his office.

Mouse zipped up Magellan's pouch and followed after.

"Come inside." Mr. Cooper unlocked the door and stepped into his office. "Close the door behind you, please."

Rebekah's heart pounded as she closed the door. He sounded very serious. She guessed that he'd already looked through her notebook.

"Mr. Cooper, I can explain." Rebekah took a deep breath.

"Explain what?" Mr. Cooper sat down behind his desk. He peered at her for a long moment. "I need to talk to you both about something, but I need to be sure that you can keep it a secret. Can I trust you, Rebekah?"

Rebekah's eyes widened. Of all the things she had expected him to say, that was not one of them. "Sure you can." She glanced at Mouse.

"You can trust me too." Mouse smiled.

"Great, because I have an idea. I want to have a special lock-in for all the students at the school—a sleepover. I thought it would be a great way to celebrate the new school and our first year together. What do you two think?"

EIGHT

"I think it's a great idea." Rebekah looked around Mr. Cooper's desk for any sign of her notebook. She glanced over the shelves and display cases packed with odd and ancient objects. None of the items were her notebook.

"Great, I could use your help with it." He looked over at Mouse. "What do you say, Mouse?"

"Sure! We'll help, Mr. Cooper." Mouse wiped some sweat from his forehead.

"Wonderful, I'll be in touch." He waved to the door. "You can go. Oh, and Rebekah?"

Rebekah paused with her hand on the doorknob. Was this the moment he'd tell her that he'd found her notebook?

"Great job looking out for Camila. She seems to really be enjoying our school."

"Thanks, Mr. Cooper." She hurried out the door. As soon as it closed, she looked at Mouse. "I don't think he had it. Do you?"

"If he does, he either didn't read it, or doesn't know it's yours." He raised an eyebrow. "Do you think that's possible?"

"Maybe." Rebekah frowned as Camila waved to her from the end of the hall. "I've got to walk Camila home."

"I have to pick up some extra homework from math class." Mouse frowned. "I might have forgotten to do a few assignments. I'll see you tomorrow?"

"Yup." Rebekah sighed.

"Try not to worry, Rebekah. We're going to find it."

"You're right, I know we will!"

Rebekah walked beside Camila along the sidewalk. She couldn't stop thinking about her notebook.

"Music club was great, thanks for telling me about it. How did your project with Mouse go?"

"Strangely." Rebekah shook her head.

"What were you and Mr. Cooper talking about? I saw you come out of his office." Camila narrowed her eyes. "Was it about the strange deliveries he's been getting?"

"No, it wasn't about that. Just something he wants Mouse and me to help him with." She paused beside Camila's house.

"Dinner tomorrow night at your house, right?" Camila smiled.

"Absolutely." Rebekah nodded.

"Great, see you tomorrow." She waved to her and headed inside.

As Rebekah walked the rest of the way to her house, something Camila said played back in her thoughts.

"The deliveries?" She took a sharp breath. "How does Camila know anything about the deliveries?"

The thought stuck with her through the night and into the next morning.

She showed up at Mouse's house early.

"Hey, Rebekah." Mouse yawned as he stood in his doorway, still in his pajamas. "What's up?"

"You said Mr. Cooper gets those deliveries early in the morning, right? I'm going to stake his office out this morning."

"You are? I thought you were looking for your notebook."

REBEKAH - GIRL DETECTIVE FIFTH GRADE MYSTERIES

"I am, but this is important too. I have a hunch." She frowned. "But you're going to have to get changed first."

"Alright, I'll be right out!"

As Rebekah waited for him, she wondered how Camila could possibly know about the deliveries. She was certain she hadn't said a word to her about them.

NINE

"Not a word to Camila about any of this, okay, Mouse?" Rebekah walked toward Camila's house at a faster pace. "Hopefully she doesn't see us."

"Not a word." Mouse nodded.

As they hurried past Camila's house, Rebekah didn't hear a door open.

She let out a breath of relief as they made it to the school without any sign of her.

"The truck usually comes in about ten minutes." Mouse checked his watch. "I'm sure we won't miss it."

"If he gets a delivery today." Rebekah pulled open the door to the school.

"He has gotten one every day, so hopefully he will. But what are we going to do once we see it?"

"Maybe we can get to it before Mr. Cooper does and have a look inside."

"Oh, Rebekah, I don't know if that's such a good idea." Mouse frowned. "What if he catches us?"

"If he has my notebook, it's not going to matter either way.

He'll already know that we're on to him." She picked out a spot not too far from Mr. Cooper's office behind a large trash can.

"But what if he doesn't?" Mouse crouched down beside her.

"Let's just see if there's even a delivery first." She peered around the trash can just in time to see Camila disappear behind a display case on the other side of Mr. Cooper's office. "What is Camila doing here?" She gasped.

"Get down, Rebekah, here comes the delivery." Mouse pulled her back down behind the trash can.

Rebekah frowned as she watched the delivery man place a small box outside of Mr. Cooper's door. He knocked once on the door, then turned and walked away.

Rebekah held her breath as she waited to see if Mr. Cooper would open the door. After a minute passed without him opening it, she looked over at Mouse. "Now's our chance. If he's not in the office, then we can get a look at it before he gets it."

"We might have to wait our turn." Mouse cringed as he pointed to Camila, who had just picked up the box.

"Camila!" Rebekah jumped out from behind the trash can. "What are you doing?"

Camila gasped and almost dropped the box. She managed to catch it before it could hit the ground.

"Rebekah, we need to see what's inside this box!" She hurried down the hall with it to the first empty classroom.

Rebekah and Mouse chased after her.

As Rebekah stepped inside the classroom, she saw Camila lift one of the flaps of the boxes.

"The tape lifted right off!" Camila smiled.

"What's inside?" Mouse walked over to her.

"Let's see." Rebekah peered into the box from the other side.

Camila lifted the packing paper and revealed a small stone circle. It was engraved with many symbols.

"What is it?" Rebekah stared at the stone. "It's beautiful."

"I know what this is." Camila's eyes widened. "There's no way Mr. Cooper should have this. It's an Aztec Sun Stone. I've seen many of these in museums back home. I don't think people can just buy them."

"If you can't just buy them, then how did Mr. Cooper get one?" Mouse frowned.

"Maybe he stole it." Rebekah raised her eyebrows. "Maybe that's why he gets his deliveries at the school instead of his house."

"We'd better put it back. Quick!" Mouse shook his head. "He's going to be looking for it."

"You're right." Camila placed the paper wrapping back in the top of the box and folded the flaps down. She smoothed the tape so that it would stay closed.

TEN

As Rebekah stepped into the hall, she saw Principal Cooper headed for his office.

"We're too late." She frowned.

"Don't worry." Mouse smiled. "I can take care of this."

Mouse unzipped Magellan's pouch and scooped the mouse out into his hand. He set Magellan down on the floor in the hallway and smiled as he ran off toward Mr. Cooper.

"Mouse!" Mr. Cooper gasped as he jumped back. "There's a mouse!"

Magellan bolted past him.

Mr. Cooper ran after him.

Mouse ran after both of them.

Rebekah and Camila ran over to Mr. Cooper's office.

"It was right here." Camila set the box down.

"Perfect." Rebekah nodded.

"Let's get out of here." Camila ran toward the hallway.

Rebekah caught her arm. "Wait a minute, we need to talk about how you knew about the deliveries and what you were doing here this morning!"

Mr. Cooper cleared his throat as he walked past the two girls.

"I don't care what it takes, I won't have mice running around my school. Get someone out here now!" Mr. Cooper barked into his cell phone. He scooped up the box, then unlocked the door to his office. As he opened the door, the flaps on the box popped open. He looked from the open box to the two girls huddled near his office. "Girls, get to class, please." Mr. Cooper frowned.

Camila pulled Rebekah down another hall. "Do you think he knows we opened it?"

"I don't know." Rebekah crossed her arms. "Do you have something to tell me?"

"Yes." Camila sighed. "I am also a detective, Rebekah—just like you. Back home, I solve all the mysteries in my town." She opened her backpack and pulled out Rebekah's notebook. "I'm sorry I took this, but I thought I could help. I hope we can still be friends."

Rebekah took her notebook. "As a fellow detective, I understand. Maybe you can help me solve the mystery of Mr. Cooper." She grinned.

"I'd like that." Camila smiled.

Later that night, at Rebekah's house, she had a special gift for Camila. "Here." She handed her the present.

"What's this for?" Camila smiled.

"If we're going to work together, you should have one of these."

Camila opened the wrapping paper and found a detective's notebook just like Rebekah's.

"Thank you so much!" Camila hugged her.

"Now you won't have to steal mine!" Rebekah laughed.

Camila opened her notebook and began to write down a few

notes. "With the two of us working together, we'll have the Principal Cooper mystery solved in no time!"

Rebekah felt a rush of excitement as she sat down next to her new friend to compare notes. She was used to solving mysteries with Mouse and sometimes her cousin, RJ, when they were together, but another true girl detective was really going to help bring her skills to another level.

She was ready for the next adventure!

BOOK 8: THE CASE OF PRINCIPAL COOPER

ONE

Rebekah looked over at her best friend, Mouse, and grinned as they both heard Camila approaching.

"Come on inside." Mouse gestured for Camila to climb up into his clubhouse.

"Nice place." She smiled as she settled onto the floor near one of the windows.

"Thanks." Mouse smiled back at her. "It's top secret."

"We're lucky he's letting us in." Rebekah winked at Camila. "Usually he uses it to plan pranks."

"Pranks? You?" Camila raised her eyebrows. "Mouse, I'm shocked."

"Ha ha." Mouse smiled. "It's all for fun."

"We're not here for fun tonight." Rebekah opened her detective's notebook and set it in on the floor in the middle of the clubhouse. "Tonight, we're here to plan."

"Yes." Camila smiled as she sat forward on her knees. "Tomorrow night is the night, right?"

"I think so." Rebekah nodded. "Principal Cooper will be busy with the lock-in tomorrow. We'll have twenty-four hours to get inside his office and find some real proof of what he is up to."

"I'm still not sure how we're going to do this without getting caught." Mouse frowned. "He always seems to be lurking nearby."

"We need to be very careful because breaking into the principal's office could get us into a lot of trouble." Camila frowned.

"If we plan ahead, we can make sure we're very careful." Rebekah pointed to a sketch on the open page of her notebook. "We know where all the different activities are happening throughout the school."

"The problem is, we need to know where Mr. Cooper will be." Mouse studied the map of activities that Rebekah had drawn. "He could be anywhere."

"So, we need to find a way to keep him in one place." Rebekah looked through the activities. "I know that most of the teachers are each running an activity. If Mr. Cooper had to run an activity, then he would be stuck in one place."

"Great idea." Mouse grinned. "But which one?"

"How about the dunk tank in the gym?" Camila pointed to the gym on Rebekah's drawing. "That will keep him pretty far away from his office, and everyone will be watching him. I'm sure it will be one of the most popular activities."

"Perfect." Rebekah nodded.

"Only one problem." Mouse frowned. "How are we going to get him to agree to be in the dunk tank? He's the principal, he can decide what he's going to do. Why would he volunteer for that?"

"We'll just have to convince him." Rebekah grinned. "I'm always up for a challenge."

"With all of those strange items and artifacts in his office, there might be a lot of people who are missing them. If Mr. Cooper really is a thief, then we're going to need a lot of proof to catch him." Camila stared down at the notebook. "Do you really think we can do it, Rebekah?"

"We have to." Rebekah snapped her notebook shut. "We're both great detectives, and with Mouse's help, there's no way we won't be able to solve this mystery."

THAT NIGHT, Rebekah thought about all of the suspicious things her principal had done since the school year had started. She had thought from the very beginning that he was different—strange even—but she'd never suspected that he might be a thief until she and Camila had caught him receiving deliveries of artifacts that belonged in museums, not on the shelves of an office.

"Whatever you're up to, Mr. Cooper, we're going to catch you!"

TWO

The next day, right after the last class, the lock-in began.

Rebekah headed straight for Mr. Cooper's office. She met him at the door, just as he stepped out into the hall.

"Well, hello, Rebekah." He laughed. "I almost bumped into you."

"I'm so excited about the lock-in." Rebekah smiled. "I already put my sleeping bag in my locker."

"That's great." He started down the hall.

"Mr. Cooper, there's something I need to talk to you about."

"Can it wait? I have a lot to get ready for tonight."

"I'm sorry, it really can't." Rebekah frowned.

"Okay then, walk with me." He continued down the hall. "What do you want to talk about?"

"I heard that you assigned Mr. Wiley to the dunk tank?" Rebekah matched his pace as they walked.

"Yes, I did. He said he didn't mind." Mr. Cooper smiled. "I bet you can't wait to get a turn to try to dunk him."

"Actually..." Rebekah frowned. "It seems a little mean, don't you think?"

"Mean? It's all for fun. Mr. Wiley knows that."

"Does he?" She raised an eyebrow. "He spends all of his time cleaning up our messes, and then we send him into the dunk tank? It feels a bit cruel to me."

"I guess I hadn't thought about it that way." Mr. Cooper stopped walking. "Do you really think that's the case?"

"It's not about what I think." She shrugged. "It's what I heard Mr. Wiley muttering earlier today. He seemed pretty upset that he'd been given the assignment."

"Oh?" Mr. Cooper sighed. "I really thought he was excited about it. I would never want him to feel forced to do it."

"Maybe you should talk to him." Rebekah smiled. "Someone else could take his place."

"All of the other teachers are already assigned." He looked at the clipboard in his hand. "And no one else was interested in that job."

"You're a great principal, Mr. Cooper, I'm sure you'll think of something." She smiled at him, then walked off down the hall.

As soon as she rounded the corner she broke into a run. She needed to get to Mr. Wiley as soon as possible.

She found him in the gym. He put a hose into the large clear tank in the middle of the gym, then walked back toward the door that led outside.

"Mr. Wiley!" She waved to him.

"Oh, hi, Rebekah. I'm a little busy right now. I need to fill up the dunk tank."

"That's what I want to talk to you about." Rebekah crossed her arms. "Did Mr. Cooper make you take this job?"

"He asked me if I would. He didn't make me."

"Really, Mr. Wiley, it's not fair for you to have to be in the dunk tank, and then also clean up the mess it makes." Rebekah shook her head. "Wouldn't it be more fun for you to be part of the pie eating contest in the cafeteria?"

"Sure, that sounds delicious." Mr. Wiley laughed. "But if I'm not in the dunk tank, who else is going to be? This is sure to be a favorite event for the kids."

"You know what would make it even more popular?" Rebekah grinned.

"What?" Mr. Wiley asked.

"If Mr. Cooper was the one in the dunk tank. All the kids would line up to get a chance to dunk the principal!"

"You're right!" He laughed. "I'm sure they would. But I don't think Mr. Cooper is going to be interested in being in the dunk tank."

"You won't know unless you ask him." Rebekah shrugged. "He's a pretty fun guy, right? He does things a little differently than most principals. I'm sure that he would go for it."

"I guess it's worth a shot." He shrugged. "And there he is now!"

THREE

Mr. Wiley pointed to Mr. Cooper headed in his direction. "Mr. Cooper!" The janitor set off down the hall toward him. "I need to speak with you!"

"I need to talk to you too." Mr. Cooper met him halfway down the hallway.

"Me first." Mr. Wiley cleared his throat. "I think it's really rotten that you assigned me to the dunk tank. I don't deserve to be treated like that!"

"I really thought you wanted to do it." Mr. Cooper frowned. "I'm sorry. I'd like to assign someone else, but everyone else already has a job."

"Everyone but you." Mr. Wiley crossed his arms. "You'd be perfect for it. The kids would love to dunk their principal! Isn't that right, Rebekah?"

"Yes, it is." Rebekah grinned. "You should do it, Mr. Cooper! It would be so much fun."

"Oh, but I didn't bring a swim suit." Mr. Cooper shook his head. "I don't have anything to wear in the dunk tank."

"That's alright, you're about my size. You can wear my swim

trunks." Mr. Wiley smiled. "Thanks, Mr. Cooper, you really put the 'pal' in principal."

"Oh, but wait!" Mr. Cooper sighed as Mr. Wiley walked off down the hall.

"I can't wait to tell everyone the news!" Rebekah ran off down the hall.

She rounded the corner and found Mouse and Camila waiting for her.

"How did it go?" Mouse grinned.

"I'm pretty sure it worked." Rebekah took a deep breath. "Camila, you were right. As soon as I put the idea in Mr. Wiley's head, he went for it."

"Great, so we can count on Mr. Cooper being in the dunk tank, but that still doesn't get us into his office." Mouse frowned. "We need his key."

"That's your job." Rebekah smiled. "Mr. Cooper will have to go into the locker room to change into his swim suit. You can go in there too. I'm sure he'll set his keys down somewhere. When he does, all you have to do is pick them up."

"Oh yes, all I have to do is steal the principal's keys." He rolled his eyes. "No big deal!"

"I would do it, but I don't think that would go over too well." Camila laughed. "You're the only boy, Mouse. You have to do it!"

"I know, I know." He shook his head. "Don't worry, I'll get those keys."

FOUR

Rebekah and Camila stood close together just outside of the gym and waited for Mouse.

"Maybe he's not going to get them." Camila frowned as she tried to peer inside.

"Don't look!" Rebekah pulled her back from the door. "We can't do anything to tip off Mr. Cooper. If he catches us, we'll never get a chance to crack this case."

"Sorry. You're right."

"Mouse will get the job done, he always does. We need to be patient."

"I guess I'm just used to working on my own." Camila nodded.

"Not this time." Rebekah winked at her. "This time you have a whole team."

The door to the gym suddenly swung open. "Here you go!" Mouse held out the keys. "But we need to make this fast. I don't know how long we'll have before Mr. Cooper figures out that they're missing."

A loud splash sounded from inside the gym, followed by several cheers.

"Oh, I think he's going to be occupied for a while." Rebekah laughed. "Let's go!"

As she led her friends down the hall to the principal's office, she was relieved to see that most of the kids and teachers were busy with the activities. Nobody seemed to notice that they weren't participating.

Rebekah slid the key into the lock and turned the knob.

"Mouse, keep watch." Rebekah stepped into the office.

Camila stepped in behind her. "It's already a little dark in here." Camila shivered. "Mr. Cooper's collection is even more creepy."

"We need evidence." Rebekah began to open the drawers in Mr. Cooper's desk. "Something that proves he's stealing these artifacts."

"Hopefully he keeps good records." Camila pulled open the drawer of a filing cabinet.

"Look! There's the book I saw before!" Rebekah pointed to a book on Mr. Cooper's desk. "Let's see what it says." She flipped the book open and thumbed through the pages inside. "I saw this once before. It's a list of the items in this office along with notes about them." She pointed to one of the entries. "This one is about that statue over there, I think. It talks about the shape of the face and the horns on it."

"I think you're right." Camila nodded. "Does it say where he stole it from?"

"No, it doesn't. It does have a number next to it though. I just don't know what the number means." She frowned. "We need to take it with us to do some more research."

"We can't take it." Camila shook her head. "Mr. Cooper will notice that it's missing. Remember when you lost your detective's notebook? You wouldn't stop looking for it."

"I didn't lose it, you took it." Rebekah raised her eyebrows.

"Right, I know. I'm sorry." Camila frowned.

"I know why you did it." Rebekah smiled. "But you're the one that's right. We can't take this book with us. But we still need the information from it."

FIVE

"I have an idea." Camila pulled her phone out of her pocket. "We can take pictures."

"Yes!" Rebekah began to turn each page in the notebook. She waited long enough for Camila to snap a picture, then turned to the next page. As she reached the last page, she noticed an outline of something underneath the thin paper.

"What's this?" Rebekah flipped the last page over and revealed a key taped to the inside of the back of the book.

"Rebekah! It's a key! I bet it will lead to the proof we need!"

"It's just a key though." Rebekah peeled it off the book. "It doesn't say what to use it for. It's about the same size as the key we used to open the door to the office."

"Then maybe it opens another door." Camila raised an eyebrow.

"The only other door is the closet." Rebekah walked over to it. She grabbed the knob of the door and looked at it. "It doesn't even have a keyhole."

"Okay, so it's not the closet." Camila turned around slowly as she looked around the office. "Maybe it opens another door?"

"There isn't another one." Rebekah shrugged.

"You know, my principal's office back home is a lot bigger than this." Camila crossed her arms.

"The principal's office at my last school was much bigger too." Rebekah narrowed her eyes.

"Do you think there could be a hidden room?" Camila frowned.

"Maybe. With Mr. Cooper it wouldn't surprise me. But where would it be? Most of the walls have shelves and display cases on them." Rebekah's eyes swept the room. "Except for that one!" She pointed at a wall where a large colorful tapestry hung.

"Good find, Rebekah!" Camila smiled. "I bet that's where the hidden door is." She walked over to the tapestry and pulled it away from the wall.

Rebekah ducked under it and felt along the wall. "I think I found something!"

"What is it?" Camila shined the light from her phone at the wall.

"A keyhole!" Rebekah laughed. "It's built right into the wall. There's no knob!"

"How strange!" Camila shook her head. "Mr. Cooper has really gone to a lot of trouble to make sure that it stays hidden. That must be where our proof is. Does the key fit?"

"Let's find out." Rebekah slid the key into the hole. "It goes in." She met Camila's eyes. "Let's see if it turns."

As she started to turn the key, the office door creaked as it swung open.

Rebekah and Camila gasped, certain that Mr. Cooper had caught them.

SIX

"Camila! Rebekah!" Mouse hissed their names. "Where are you?"

"We're here." Rebekah sighed with relief as she poked her head out from behind the tapestry. "We found a key and a hidden door. We're close to finding out the truth about Principal Cooper!"

"Speed it up," Mouse said. "He could come back at any time! We have to hurry."

"We will!" Rebekah frowned. "Just don't scare us like that again!"

"Sorry." Mouse cringed. "Open the door so we can get out of here." He closed the office door behind him as he stepped back into the hall.

"Go on, Rebekah. Try the key," Camila said.

Rebekah turned the key. It twisted easily, and she heard the sound of a lock opening.

"It opened!" Camila grinned. "Let's see what's inside." She pushed her hands against the door.

The door didn't budge.

"Is it stuck?" Rebekah frowned. She pushed her hands against the door as well. It still didn't move.

"Maybe there's another lock?" Camila pointed her flashlight at the wall in search of another keyhole.

"Wait, look at this." Rebekah pointed to the floor. "There's dust everywhere but where we stepped and right in front of the door. Maybe it slides open?" She tried to slide the door to the side.

The door slid almost all the way into the wall.

Camila pointed her flashlight through the door. "It's another room!"

"Just as big as the office." Rebekah peered inside. "With just as many statues and artifacts!"

"Wow, look at this." Camila pointed her flashlight at a ruby statue of a monkey that glittered in the light.

"It's beautiful." Rebekah smiled. "No wonder he has it hidden."

"There's more." Camila ran the flashlight beam along the entire shelf. All of the statues were different animals in an assortment of different colors. "An elephant, an eagle—look, there's even a mouse." She swung her flashlight through the darkness. "I wonder what else he has in here."

"There aren't any windows. There's no way for light to get in." Rebekah frowned. "There must be a light switch somewhere."

"Even if there is, we probably shouldn't turn it on." Camila looked over at her. "We shouldn't touch too much, actually. If Mr. Cooper went to all of this trouble to hide these things, he might have some kind of alarm set up."

"You're right." Rebekah frowned at the thought. "We might have even set it off already. We need to find some proof and get out of here fast."

"Where should we look?" Camila pointed the light at the display cases and shelves. "I don't see any more books in here."

"There has to be something." Rebekah felt along the wall behind one of the shelves. "Maybe he hid something in the wall."

Camila swung the flashlight around again. As the beam flashed across the wall near the ceiling, a pair of large eyes glowed. They looked straight at Rebekah and Camila.

SEVEN

Camila let out a shriek as she jumped back and bumped into one of the display cases.

"Shh!" Rebekah gasped and looked toward the door. She held her breath as she waited to see if Mr. Cooper would burst through it.

"What is that?" Camila whispered as she pointed the flashlight at the eyes again.

"I'm not sure." Rebekah peered up at it. "But I don't think it's real." Rebekah pulled out her phone and turned her flashlight on as well. She pointed it straight at the eyes. With both lights on them, the eyes became more visible, as did the golden frame around them. "It's some kind of large mask." Rebekah sighed. "And the eyes are glowing because they're made of gemstones. The light reflected off of them." She looked over at Camila. "That got us pretty good, didn't it?"

"It sure did." Camila shook her head. "I think we'd better get out of here."

"We can't. Not yet." Rebekah frowned. "We haven't found any proof. We have to keep looking."

"We have to hurry!" Camila ran the beam of her flashlight

around the room again. "There!" Camila pointed the light at a pile of papers on a corner of one of the shelves. "Those look like receipts of some kind. Maybe they will show where he purchased these items from. If we can find out who he bought them from, we might be able to prove that the purchase was illegal."

"Good idea." Rebekah picked up the pile of receipts. "They're hand-written." She squinted in the darkness. "I can't really read them."

"Is this better?" Camila aimed the light at the papers.

"Not really, I think they're in another language." She sighed.

"Should we take pictures of them?" Camila switched her phone to camera mode.

"We don't have time. If Mr. Cooper catches us in here, he might decide to make us part of his collection." Rebekah shivered at the thought. "I'm just going to have to take them with me. Maybe we can find a way to translate them." She slipped the stack of receipts into her pocket, then took one last look around the room. "We really should go."

"Okay." Camila patted her shoulder. "Don't worry, Rebekah, we're going to catch him."

"I just hope he doesn't catch us." Rebekah stepped back through the door and pushed the tapestry away from the wall. Once Camila stepped out, she slid the door to the secret room closed. She turned the key to make sure it was locked.

"We have to put this back. If he finds out its missing, he'll know someone was in there." She walked back over to the book on the desk and taped the key back inside it.

Suddenly they heard a flurry of knocks on the office door.

"Oh no!" Camila gasped. "That's Mouse's signal that Mr. Cooper is coming!"

EIGHT

Rebekah rushed up to the door and peeked out through the small opening. She spotted Mr. Cooper and Mouse right in front of the door and she strained to be able to hear what they were saying.

Mr. Cooper's t-shirt and swim trunks were dripping water all over the floor.

"Mouse, I need to get into my office." He frowned. "What are you doing out here anyway? With all of the fun activities going on, you're hanging out in the hallway?"

"Oh, I just needed a break from all the fun." Mouse laughed. "You know, too much of a good thing can really wear you out."

"I see. Well, I need to get into my office, so if you don't mind, can you step aside?"

"Mr. Cooper, I didn't get a turn to dunk you. You're not done already, are you?"

Rebekah grabbed Camila's arm. "We have to find somewhere to hide. I don't think we'll be able to get out of here."

"Where?" Camila gasped.

"There's only one place!" Rebekah ran back to the notebook

269

on the desk. She peeled the key from the back of it again and passed it over to Camila.

Camila ran behind the tapestry that hung on the wall. She unlocked the door and slid it open.

Rebekah peered through the crack in the door once more. "Maybe Mouse distracted him."

She looked through just in time to see Mr. Cooper with his hand on Mouse's shoulder, guiding him away from the door to the office.

Rebekah gulped and ran behind the tapestry and through the secret door.

Camila slid the door halfway shut, just before the door to the office swung open.

"It's a good thing I left this unlocked. Although it's strange that I did. When I went into the locker room, I realized that I had forgotten my phone in here. Then I couldn't find my keys." He cleared his throat. "I guess you wouldn't know anything about that, Mouse, would you?"

"No sir, not at all." Mouse gulped.

Rebekah held her breath and listened so hard that she heard the sound of Mouse unzipping Magellan's pouch. Her heart pounded as she looked over at Camila. She guessed that Mouse's plan was to distract the principal by letting Magellan loose in his office. Maybe that would give them enough time to escape.

"Be ready." She whispered to Camila.

Camila nodded.

Rebekah heard the scratch of Magellan's nails against the office's wooden floor.

"Mouse!" Mouse shouted with a high-pitched shriek. "There's a mouse, Mr. Cooper!"

Rebekah grabbed Camila's hand. Her heart pounded as she waited to hear Mr. Cooper run out of the office.

NINE

"Oh, a mouse, huh?" Mr. Cooper chuckled as he chased after the mouse.

Mouse gasped as Mr. Cooper easily scooped the mouse up into his hands. "Mr. Cooper! Please don't hurt him!"

Rebekah squeezed Camila's hand.

"His name is Magellan, right?" Mr. Cooper's voice carried past the tapestry.

Rebekah's eyes widened. How did Mr. Cooper know the name of Mouse's pet?

"Yes, it is." Mouse sighed. "He's my pet, Mr. Cooper. Please don't hurt him or take him away."

"I'm not going to hurt him." Mr. Cooper laughed. "Why would you think that? He's a cute little mouse. He must be very smart too, because you're always sending him on adventures, aren't you? Do you think I haven't noticed that it's always the same mouse that gets loose in this school, and you're always around when it happens?" He laughed again. "You must really think I don't pay attention."

"I'm sorry, Mr. Cooper. I didn't mean to cause any trouble. Can I have him back please?"

"Oh, you'll get him back—when you start telling me the truth." Mr. Cooper sighed. "I'm assuming you're the one that stole my keys. I'm sure Rebekah wouldn't have gone into the boys' locker room."

"I—uh." Mouse coughed.

"And, if you were hanging out in the hallway, I'd guess that you were acting as the lookout." Mr. Cooper cleared his throat. "Which means that Rebekah is hiding in here somewhere, isn't she?"

Rebekah's heart dropped. She looked over at Camila.

Camila frowned.

"No, of course not." Mouse gasped.

The tapestry suddenly whipped out from in front of the hidden door and Mr. Cooper stared straight into Rebekah's eyes.

"Don't you think you'd better come out here now, Rebekah?"

Rebekah took a sharp breath. "Mr. Cooper, I can explain."

Mr. Cooper slid the door back and revealed Camila.

"Camila?" He raised his eyebrows. "Now, that I didn't expect."

"I bet you didn't!" Camila put her hands on her hips. "I bet you hoped that no one would ever find out about your stolen artifacts! But we did! It doesn't matter if you caught us. We know the truth!"

"What?" Mr. Cooper handed Magellan over to Mouse, then stared at each of the girls in front of him. "What are you talking about?"

"This." Rebekah pulled the receipts out of her pocket. "We know that you've been getting deliveries of stolen artifacts. These objects belong in museums, Mr. Cooper! You can't just keep them for yourself!"

Mr. Cooper let out a big breath, then looked up at the ceiling. "What am I going to do? Of all of the schools in the world, I had to pick the one with Rebekah, the girl detective."

"Camila's a detective too!" Rebekah glared at him. "You never stood a chance!"

"Oh, wonderful. Just what I need—two of you." He shook his head and it looked like he was trying to keep from laughing. "What am I going to do with you?"

TEN

"It doesn't matter what you do to us, Mr. Cooper, we'll make sure the truth gets out." Rebekah frowned.

"But we really wouldn't make good additions to your collection." Camila shivered. "It might be better if you just let us go."

"Sit down. All of you." He pointed to the chairs in front of his desk. "Now."

Rebekah glanced at Camila, then at Mouse, who slipped Magellan back into his pouch. Then she sat down in one of the chairs. They'd already been caught; she at least wanted to hear what Mr. Cooper had to say.

Once all three of them were seated, Mr. Cooper walked behind his desk. Water continued to drip from his hair as he looked at them.

"I really admire your intelligence and determination, but this has gotten way out of hand. Being a great detective is a very important job, but you have to make sure that when you accuse someone of something, they are actually guilty of it." He held out his hand to Rebekah. "My key, please."

Rebekah placed the key to the hidden door in his hand.

He put it back inside the book, then sat down in his chair.

"The truth is, I used to be an archaeologist." He pulled a picture from the desk drawer and set it on the table for them to see.

Rebekah leaned forward, her curiosity getting the best of her as Mr. Cooper continued to speak.

"I spent all my time digging through ancient ruins and finding the most interesting and beautiful things. Some of those things were given to me, because people trusted me to take good care of them. I've traveled the whole world and learned so much that I decided I wanted to share what I learned. So, I became a principal. When I came here, I brought my collection with me. But I couldn't bring everything at once, so some of the items have been shipped to me." He raised an eyebrow. "I'm guessing that made you think that they were stolen."

Rebekah and Camila looked at one another and sunk down in their seats a bit.

He sighed. "I've never stolen anything. Those receipts you have are from many different countries. They all contain the promise that I will only display the items and not sell them or use them for profit. I've been eager to share them with all of you. But I've also been concerned that something might get broken."

Rebekah cringed as she recalled Camila bumping into the display case. Maybe Mr. Cooper was right to keep them hidden away.

"Oh—uh—wow, we're sorry Mr. Cooper." Rebekah frowned.

"You could have asked. I've told you that so many times. I've tried to be patient, but this time, you three could have destroyed some very valuable artifacts." He shook his head. "I can't let that happen."

"We didn't hurt anything." Mouse's eyes widened.

"But you could have. I thought my collection would be safe here, but now I see that it's not." He sighed.

"Maybe, instead of locking it away, you could have a special assembly—where everyone can see a few of the items at a time and you could tell us your stories about finding them." Rebekah met his eyes. "I know everyone would love that. Camila, Mouse, and I can make sure that everything stays safe. Now that we know the truth, we can help you keep your collection safe!"

"You'd do that?" He smiled. "Even for someone strange and creepy like Mr. Cooper?"

"You're not so strange after all." Rebekah laughed. "But maybe a little weird."

"Weird is a good thing!" Mouse grinned.

"Let's give it a try." Mr. Cooper nodded. "Now, there's the matter of how to punish you for stealing my keys and breaking into my office."

"Detention forever." Mouse groaned.

Rebekah winced.

Camila sighed.

"Oh, no. I have something else in mind."

Minutes later Rebekah squeezed her eyes shut and held her breath just before she crashed down into the water of the dunk tank. She sputtered as she came back up to the surface.

Mouse shrieked with laughter as he pointed at her.

"Keep laughing!" She grinned. "You're next!"

Rebekah felt proud that she'd finally cracked the case of Principal Cooper. Once again, she hadn't been exactly right, but the end result was much more fun that she'd imagined.

The fact that she had a fellow detective as her new friend held so much promise for the adventures that were sure to continue in the year ahead.

Yes, fifth grade was proving to be one challenging mystery after another.

And Rebekah, girl detective, was ready for it all!

ALSO BY PJ RYAN

Amazon.com/author/pjryan

*Visit the author page to save big on special bundled sets!

AVAILABLE IN AUDIO

PJ Ryan books for kids are also available as audiobooks.

Visit the author website for a complete list at: PJRyanBooks.com

You can also listen to free audio samples there.

Made in the USA
Las Vegas, NV
20 November 2022

59654394R00166